# MY SEVENTH SUMMER

*Tale of a Sheepman's Daughter*

by

Eve Crane Dayton

*The Bill & Lula Crane family*
*Back row (l-r): Daddy, Mama, Wilma, Karen, Tim.*
*Middle: Norene, Ginger, Eve, Melvin.*
*Front: Laurence, McKay. (Louise taking photo)*

# ENDORSEMENTS

"In addition to a brilliant portrayal of life on a family ranch in mid-20th century, Eve Dayton has cleverly contrived an intriguing mystery that will keep you guessing until the very end "

*—Sharon Rowsell Warner*

"This is a heartfelt book that will bring a longing for bygone days to the depths of your soul. The wonders of childhood are brought to life in this book."

*—Lana Tippetts Foy*

"Children become responsible adults by learning to work. Eve Crane and her nine siblings did chores from a young age and were guided around the dinner table. Every evening their father called upon each child to share something on their mind. *My Seventh Summer* is a primer on how to raise children, all the while telling a clever and touching story for all ages.

*–Lee Roderick, author, journalist, former*
*President,* National Press Club

"As a child I knew 'Evie' Crane and her incredible family. Her parents were every bit 'the good shepherds' along with a lot of other good shepherds you will find in this book."

*—Margaret Payne Broadbent*

"Within these pages Evie's mom and dad teach us what true parenting is all about—nurturing the human soul."

*—Yvonne Maddox Roderick, former*
*Mother of the Year, American Mother's Inc.*

"Eve Dayton's rare ability to see the world through the eyes of her seven-year-old self growing up on a sheep ranch in a family of ten children in the 1950's is remarkable! This book made me laugh and cry. It is fun, engaging, and a vivid reminder of the treasure of parents teaching their children the most important values of life. It is a book for all ages! I look forward to reading it aloud with my grandchildren this summer!"

*—Linda Jacobson Eyre, co-creator,*
*Joy Schools and GrandParenting 101*

# MY SEVENTH SUMMER

## *Tale of a Sheepman's Daughter*

by

Eve Crane Dayton

Edited by
Lee Roderick

PROBITAS PRESS
Los Angeles Phoenix Washington D.C.

PROBITAS PRESS
Los Angeles



Published in the United States by Probitas Press, LLC, Los Angeles



Library of Congress Control Number: 2023938236

Publisher's Cataloging-in-Publication Data
Names: Dayton, Eve Crane, 1947-2022, author. | Roderick, Lee, editor.
Title: My seventh summer : tale of a sheepman's daughter / by Eve Crane Dayton ; edited by Lee Roderick.
Description: Los Angeles, CA : Probitas Press, 2023. | Includes 37 b&w photos. | Audience: Ages 12+.
Identifiers: LCCN 2023938236 | ISBN 9798988281207 (pbk.) | ISBN 9798988281214 (ebook) | ISBN 979-8-9882812-2-1 (hardback)
Subjects: CYAC: Families -- Fiction. | Sheep ranches -- Fiction. | Christian life -- Fiction. | Idaho – Fiction. | LCGFT: Domestic fiction. | Christian fiction. | Detective and mystery fiction. | BISAC: YOUNG ADULT FICTION / Lifestyles / Farm & Ranch Life. | YOUNG ADULT FICTION / Historical / United States / 20th Century. | YOUNG ADULT FICTION / Religious / Christian / General.
Classification: LCC PZ7.1 D39 2023 | DDC [Fic] --dc22
LC record available at https://lccn.loc.gov/2023938236

Cover Art: *From the Garden* Courtesy of RobertDuncanStudios.com
Formatting by Mickey Fryer, MightyFineDesigns.com

*My Seventh Summer* is a delightful and mysterious adventure of an imaginative child growing up on a large family sheep ranch in 1950s' Idaho.

Probitaspress.com 800-616-8081 Fax 323-953-9850
2016 Cummings Los Angeles CA 90027
Amazon.com ymaddox@probitaspress.com

Printed in the United States of America
10 9 8 7 6 5 4 3 2

Eve Crane Dayton
dedicated this book to
Her Beloved Father and Mother
William B. and Lula Crane

Her Adored Siblings
Karen, Louise, Wilma, Tim,
Ginger, Melvin, Norene,
McKay and Laurence

Her Eternal Companion
Mark Taylor Dayton and their
Cherished Children
Cathy and Brad Martin
Cindy and Benjamin Bishop
Rachael and Chad Eberhardt
Reed and Courtney Dayton
Baby John (deceased)

"The ultimate goal of farming is not the growing of crops, but the cultivation and perfection of human beings."

—*Masanobu Fukuoka*

*The herd and their shepherd.*

## CONTENTS

*Brother Tim with sister Evie Crane, age 7.*

# INTRODUCTION

by
Linda Jacobson Eyre

Eve Crane Dayton was born to write! For decades she has delighted her family and friends with the humor and insight of her stories and her unique way of seeing the world. Being a middle child in a family of ten children made her strong and resilient, gritty and keenly observant, as well as creative.

Reading this book will either tug at your heart with warm memories of your own childhood or plunge you into a world of wonder of farm life in the 1950s that you could never have imagined. Such impressions are what a good book is all about.

The idyllic childhood of the delightful young narrator mirrors much of Eve's early life and gives no hint that her adult life was full and overflowing with challenges. To name just a few, she lost a full-term newborn baby and a 14-year-old granddaughter, fought a valiant fight with breast cancer and won. She agonized over enormous health issues with other grandchildren and supported her wonderful husband Mark, who passed away in 2018 after a long illness. After each challenge she was still a soul full of determination, optimism, and faith—lessons learned as a child from her remarkable parents.

Schooled in journalism, Eve had written many short stories and newspaper articles. But her dream was to write books. During the Covid-19 pandemic, alone in her sweet humble home in rural Bennington, Idaho, she decided it would be a perfect time to write books without interruptions of the outside world. She woke up every morning, relishing another day to pour out the new stories that had been ruminating in her imagination far too long.

Knowing little about how to format a book, she painstakingly figured it out and began writing. After the worst of the pandemic had passed, Eve emerged with five books! She began sharing her tales with her four beautiful children, their spouses, her siblings and close friends. Not knowing any other way to do it, her first books were doggedly formatted, copied page by page, and bound with spiral bindings at the local newspaper office in nearby Montpelier. Her pipe dream was that someday she might be able to publish one of her stories.

By the first part of 2022 Eve slowed down and was not feeling well. She was going to the hospital regularly for injections to increase her energy, which didn't help much. Although her condition was worsening, she stoically dealt with it. No one realized how sick she was until she could no longer get out of bed. In July she was rushed by ambulance to a regional hospital where she was diagnosed with stage four colon cancer and given only a few weeks to live.

She was lovingly cared for by a son and daughter-in-law who lived next door and reflected the same outcomes of good parenting that Eve explains in her book. I had memorable opportunities to sit with Eve during those last few weeks as we talked about her wonderful life. I asked which book she would most like to have published if she had the opportunity.

It was this one.

A few days later, loving hands tucked her into bed and she was told that, through several unexpected miracles, a publisher had been found for her book. Visibly sedated, she smiled a huge smile and drifted off to sleep, passing away on August 28, 2022.

So now you know the rest of the story!

Profound thanks to Yvonne Maddox, Lee Roderick, and Probitas Press for being part of the miracle and for seeing the beauty of this story and the joy it will bring to so many.

*Bill Crane's Brand +C*

## FOREWORD

by
Polly June Crane Willardson

This delightful tale comprises a collection and expansion of many day-to-day scenes from Eve Crane Dayton's real childhood home and family life in rural southeastern Idaho during the 1950s. Her humble, hard-working parents, William B. and Lula Crane, raised ten children who worked and played together in a home filled with love and laughter.

Eve's fictionalized story takes place in the very real setting of Bennington, Idaho and in the canyons and fields northeast of town where they grew crops and raised sheep. Eve's perspective is that of her seven-year-old self. Family personalities are drawn from her parents and nine real-life siblings: Karen, Louise, Wilma, Tim, Ginger, Melvin, Norene, McKay and Laurence. (Sibling's names have been changed in Eve's story.)

Eve has woven family memories into a summer mystery–intertwined with the demanding daily routines common on farms. Family farms, an essential slice of American history, have been often overlooked and underappreciated. After World War II, before more sophisticated farm machinery was invented, vibrant farm families toiled endlessly, quietly growing food and raising livestock for their own needs and for other households across the nation.

Sheep herds were a large part of the Crane family's life. Their modest cash income depended upon Eve's father sending hundreds of sheep to market at the end of each summer.

Readers without the opportunity to explore canyons and creeks in the back of a red pickup or on the back of a horse or mule will step into a world of wonder. Caring for farm animals, fending off predators, doing endless chores, and being taught the most important values of life by wise parents were all important parts of Eve's childhood.

Along with many siblings to interact with, Eve's creative mind also gave her an imaginary friend. Sam was a wise counselor and herder for her imaginary flock of sheep—a faithful friend who helped her process experiences and solve problems. He provided comfort when she was troubled or afraid and exulted with Eve in moments of triumph.

Get ready to be astonished by the responsibilities and hard work expected of children of this era, including helping their fathers clear land for cultivating by removing rocks or burning giant piles of uprooted sagebrush. It was a world where rural kids raised their own lambs and made their own clothes for 4-H projects. Before the day of electronic games, cell phones and social media, young people actually talked to each other face to face, built bridges across creeks, or took refuge in magic-kingdom tree houses.

Readers are about to step into the fascinating world of a young child not only full of imagination and curiosity, but also dealing with worries and sadness not unlike those sometimes faced by children today. Eve's story is a timely reminder that love is the key to seeing one safely through tough moments in all families, then or now, with one child or ten.

## PREFACE

It was a pleasant thing to be seven. I was big enough to go most places and do lots of things, yet I wasn't considered one of the little kids. My status was perfect. I was big when I wanted the benefits, but sort of small if there were really hard things to do.

I could weave in and out of whichever deal suited me best.

I didn't mean to be manipulative. I just wanted to be able to do the things I loved and avoid the things I didn't love. Was that so different from what most people, even adults, try to do?

*—Eve Crane Dayton, 2022*

*Family dinner hour with Mama, Daddy, and ten youngsters in the Crane kitchen.*

# 1

# A SECRET FRIEND

It was the beginning of summer 1954. We all sat at the table, the center of our family discussions. Daddy was at the head of the table and Mama at the other end near the stove. All ten of us kids were seated at our assigned places getting ready to eat potatoes, lamb chops and white creamy gravy—our favorite meal.

As usual there was some commotion as one of the little ones tipped over a glass of water and we waited for Mama to wipe off the red checkered oilcloth before the blessing on the food.

After "amen" we all dug in.

Daddy usually told us interesting tales of what he had been doing that day on the farm. But this time he asked me how my imaginary sheepherder Sam Hale was doing. Everyone waited for my answer.

I said Sam was doing just fine and had moved my sheep closer to home. It seemed as though everyone from my oldest sister to my baby brother were spellbound as my little girl mind ran wild with stories of my imaginary sheep ranch and all its doings. Just seeing their interest in my tales seemed to fuel the flame of my imagination.

Sometimes even I wasn't sure if the stories that came to my mind were real or not. But when prompted, an exciting new story would always tumble out. Daddy encouraged my run-away yarns. And each question he asked opened another door to part of my story. The more he egged me on, the bigger the story grew until it became my pseudo reality. So I wasn't sure the actual story began that evening, but the telling of the story saw its genesis at that very meal.

Sam, my herder, always wore a plaid flannel shirt, blue denim pants and high lace-up leather shoes. When I asked why his shoes reached so high, he said they protected him from low things like snakes, rocks, and brush. I knew he was right. Sam was always right and smart and, above all, brave. He was a hard worker and even though I was just a sprig of a kid with freckles and long braids, he managed my herd of sheep and was always kind to me. He knew more than I did about most things. But he knew the herd was mine and he was *my* sheep herder.

I didn't see Sam's wife often. Occasionally Mary came by in a black car with big square fenders and a running board on each side. She never got out. He always walked over and talked to her through the open car window. Then he took off his dusty hat with the oily sweatband, leaned through the window and gave her a kiss. I didn't like to see kisses generally, but it made me happy that he loved her. Then she would drive away in a cloud of dust and he would smile as he put his hat back on.

Everything seemed so easy and pleasant with Sam. He often chewed on a little straw twig or stem as he went about fixing the corral fences or replacing the rivets on the leather straps on his saddle bags. His horse and dog were never more than a few feet from him no matter what he was doing. He was industrious and busy and gave the appearance of serenity. I was glad he was my herder and didn't work for anyone else.

One morning after breakfast I hurried out to the corrals to see if Sam was there and what he was doing. I couldn't find him so I ran back to the barnyard and looked in the barn and surrounding buildings. I called his name, but he didn't answer. Sam's dog Tuffy and his horse Old Kit were gone too. Well that made sense because they were always with him wherever he went. I ran back to the corral and climbed up the highest pole to see if I could spot him, but he was nowhere to be seen. I thought maybe he had gone to check on the sheep. Spring was here and the ewes and their new lambs were hungry for the fresh green shoots coming up from the earth.

The herd was grazing three miles north of our house at the mouth of Sage Canyon, land my father owned. Sam asked if it was okay to put my herd there and Daddy said it would be fine as long as he watched them closely. The coyotes are everywhere up there and often killed lambs. It was also important the sheep didn't come out of the canyon and get into the green alfalfa field where the new hay crop was just starting to grow.

So Sam was busy protecting the sheep from the coyotes and protecting the crops from the sheep. It made me wonder at the great knowledge of the Creator to have such a fine balance in common things. But my mind went back to Sam. Where was he? Usually he told Daddy or me whenever he left our place to return to the sheep.

I couldn't ride the bike all the way to Sage Canyon. It had a broken pedal which made it next to impossible to use. My brother Jim, two years older than me, put a big bolt on the pedal apparatus where the foot piece was missing. It worked for short rides but was not a perfect fix and made my foot sore when I rode far. It was an old blue bike we all shared and was nearly worn out. My only other chance to go to Sage Canyon to look for Sam was if Daddy went out to his fields and I could ride with him in his red truck.

I remembered the day a year or two earlier when Daddy first brought the truck home. He pulled into the barnyard and honked the horn. We all went running out the back screen door, pigtails and rooster tails flying, to see it. How it shone in the afternoon sun! I had never seen such a bright red color. The rubber tires were black and clean. We squealed with delight when Daddy said it was ours now for the whole family to use. We climbed onto the running boards and into the bed. We climbed in and out, over and over again like ants on an ant hill trying to soak in the wonder of it all. Mama came out the back door, wiping her hands on her apron, smiling at the scene. Even though the truck carried a debt, she knew it was necessary for the farm as she and Daddy provided for their big family.

The truck lived up to its purpose, making trips back and forth to the fields every day. On this particular day I was hoping Daddy would let me ride with him so I could check on Sam and my own herd. Several of us kids rode in the back of the truck on the way to the fields.

What a beautiful day it was! School was just out for the summer, everything was in blossom and beginning to grow. The sound of meadowlarks was in the air everywhere and the buttercup field was a sea of yellow. Daddy actually named one of his sections the "Buttercup Field," because each spring it was a veritable carpet of yellow wildflowers. All you could see was yellow for about two weeks as they bloomed between the sagebrush. It was glorious!

As we bumped along the gravel road to the fields, we laughed and enjoyed our sibling camaraderie riding in the back of the truck. What joy it was to have siblings in every adventure. In our big family there was always someone by my side. But on this day my mind kept turning to Sam and my herd. As we approached the lane to the canyon, Daddy slowed down to study the order of things in his fields.

I saw some of the sheep that came down to the gate at the mouth of the canyon. The others were a little higher on the side hill grazing. It was still cool enough in the morning hours for them to enjoy nibbling. As the sun grew warmer, they would shade up through the heat of the day and then graze again toward evening. But I couldn't see Sam anywhere.

Then Daddy turned up the lane and stopped at the gate to the canyon fence. He kept his foot on the brake while Jim jumped out and opened the gate. We drove through and waited again as he closed the gate. We meandered up the rutted road at a snail's pace as Daddy looked everything over. The smell of pine, sage, and all the earth coming into itself filled our nostrils. The sheep watched curiously as we passed them by, content and not alarmed.

Then I saw Sam! He was riding up the road behind the truck on Old Kit. He wore a brown plaid shirt, smiling from ear to ear. He was chewing on a long hay stem. Tuffy was at his horse's heels as usual. Sam rode alongside the truck, all the while smiling at us kids. Then he waved, winked at me, and reined the horse up the hillside nearer my herd as we drove around a bend and out of his sight. I knew by his wink that my herd was okay and all was well. As I was turning back around I saw a blue figure moving through the trees above us. Was I the only one who saw it?

When we reached Daddy's old homestead cabin he stopped the truck and turned the motor off. That was our signal to jump out and play. He liked to check the cabin frequently to make sure the windows and doors were still tight and no skunks or rats had gotten in. The door was never locked and it opened with a gentle nudge. We poured in and mulled around for a few minutes, looking at the old wood stove, bare bed springs, table and chairs and empty wood box. Daddy looked around the old corrals and barn that had been there for twenty years, since his homesteading days. They weren't used much anymore, but he liked to have things in good repair.

I imagined he had invited Sam and Mary to live in the cabin at one time, but Sam declined, saying Mary liked to be closer to town and had a part-time job at the library. They had a little apartment in town. I think she liked town life better because whenever I happened to see her she wore a nice dress and a wide-brimmed hat with flowers around the band. She seemed less suited to ranch living than Sam. But I thought she looked quite pretty in her big hat and nice car whenever she drove out to our place to talk to Sam.

After about an hour Daddy called us to load up so we all came running from the hills and trees to the truck, our hands filled with discoveries of the day. I had pine cones and some dandy rocks.

My two oldest sisters, Kari and Lucy, were young teenagers and stayed home to help Mama that morning. That left Wendy, Jim, myself, Ginny, Mason, Nancy, Mack and Little Larry to go on the trip to the canyon. Oh, and my name is Evie. Actually my given name is Eve, but at home I was always called Evie and so it stuck. I didn't mind.

Sometimes we fought over who got to ride in the cab of the truck with Daddy, but on a day like this when the world was just coming alive we delighted at being in the back soaking up every possible sight, sound and smell. We especially liked it when Daddy drove slow. As he scrutinized the fields with his arm on the window sill, we chattered happily in the back and showed each other our collection of nature's gifts. The fresh air filled us as we bounced along.

We had the whole summer ahead of us. What could be a happier feeling? I loved the red truck. I loved our family. I loved that Sam was watching my herd of sheep, keeping them safe. I glanced back toward Sage Canyon but it was nearly out of sight. Then I saw in the pines above the sage a strange flash of blue. Was I the only one who saw it?

When we got home Mama had dinner ready for us. At our house dinner was the meal in the middle of the day and supper was the evening meal. It wasn't until years later that we kids learned most of the world calls the middle meal lunch and the evening meal dinner. But in our world, dinner was the daytime meal. And after working with our dad and siblings in the fields, we were hungry! We washed the dark canyon dirt from our hands and faces and presented ourselves at the table.

Kari and Lucy helped Mama make a delicious meal of scalloped potatoes with chunks of ham. For dessert they baked some apples. In those years we didn't have an electric stove—just a cast iron wood-burning cook stove, so it was pretty much a guess at how hot the oven was when we wanted to bake something. They cut the cores out and Mama covered them with a cinnamon and sugar syrup. As they baked the flavor seeped into them. They were delicious and we particularly loved to pour a little milk in our bowl with the hot apple when we ate them.

After eating, Wendy and I washed the dishes. Wendy was about ten and I adored everything about her. She was capable and strong and taught me many things through the years. Even though I was three or four years younger, she always treated me as an equal and stood by me when things got tough. We both wore our hair in braids, hers were dark brown and mine were a lighter brown. We stood together at the sink facing the huge challenge of all those dishes while the little girls, Ginny and Nancy, cleared the table.

The younger kids ran outside to play and the big girls were working on some 4-H project in the living room where the sewing machine was set up. As Wendy and I washed and rinsed the dishes, I could hear Mama and Daddy mention something about Sam. I kept working but perked up my ears to try to catch what Daddy was saying. Then his tone got lower and they walked out the back door together, deep in conversation.

When Mama returned she was alone. Daddy went back to the fields to continue his spring planting. Mama warmed milk on the stove and filled the lamb bottles for the bum lambs. She insisted we call them "pet" lambs because "bum" was not a nice word, so to us they were pet lambs. We took the dozen or so bottles (old empty pop bottles with black nipples) outside to the makeshift pens in the barnyard and made sure each pet lamb got some nice warm milk.

The pet lambs were cast-offs, runts or orphans whose mothers died giving birth and had to be bottle-fed to keep them alive. It became a project that produced a little cash at the end of the summer if we took good care of them so they would grow and stay healthy. But they had to be fed at least three times a day. No one was exempt from helping. Like with most duties in a big family, we all worked together.

As the lambs slobbered and chewed on my knuckles waiting their turn on the bottle, I was wondering what Daddy said to Mama about Sam. Daddy always encouraged me to tell him about Sam so I knew it couldn't be bad. Curiosity grew in me.

Day faded into evening. There was the enchanting scent of lilacs in the yard. Early every June the lilac bushes burst with blossoms. The fragrance was intoxicating. We tossed a ball in the front yard and played tag and ran foot races and spent our energy reveling in the joy of childhood. I wondered if heaven could ever be more wonderful than a summer night in our yard with loved ones all around.

As the sun dropped behind the western peaks, Mama called for us to come in. Reluctantly we obeyed, hating to leave our fun. But we knew warm baths and clean sheets awaited us beyond the screen door, so we went in. After all, tomorrow was another day soon to come and who knew what adventures it might hold for us. Daddy came in the back door after finishing his work for the day. He was as happy as the rest of us to be home together. I smiled as he sat on a kitchen chair and unlaced his high-top shoes. They were just like Sam's.

*Daddy visiting Slim and Beatrice.*

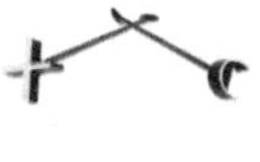

## 2

## SLIM, BEATRICE AND THE HERDS

Next morning we awoke to the aroma of bacon in the air. We dressed and like every other morning gathered at the kitchen table for the delicious meal that awaited us at the hands of dear Mama.

After prayer and we were eating, Daddy struck up the usual conversation, asking each of us about the doings in our little worlds. He was pleased the big girls started their 4-H sewing projects, that the little boys filled the wood box as they were supposed to do, and that the little girls were helpful to Mama yesterday.

Although there were ten of us he focused on each of us individually. He turned his attention my way and asked how my herd was doing and what Sam was up to these days. I assured him the sheep were fine. But I wondered about his question about Sam. Was it a simple question or was it an introduction to something he thought was not right with my invisible friend? I half-heartedly said Sam was fine too. But my young mind raced with worry.

Following breakfast, assignments were made for the day's tasks. To my joy Jim, Wendy and I were chosen to go with Daddy to see Slim at his camp way high up Sage Canyon. Slim was the nickname for Daddy's sheep herder, Epiphanial Saldani, a Mexican-American who spoke limited broken English. You can see why everyone called him Slim. He was married to a woman named Beatrice. I had only seen them a few times, but Daddy raved about the good work Slim did. I suppose he was nearly as good as Sam. But on this day, Daddy needed to talk to Slim, so he was making the journey to their camp.

We took the truck with two horses and a mule tied behind all the way to the Sage Canyon gate, about three miles away. The animals trotted along behind the slow-moving truck. I couldn't imagine trotting that far without tiring, but Daddy explained more than once that horses can trot many, many miles without tiring. We went as far as the homestead cabin where we left the truck and mounted the horses and mule. Daddy rode Sundance, a small palomino pony he was training. Jim rode Pomp, an older pinto we had for years. Wendy and I rode double on Charlie the mule.

Charlie doubled as a pack animal when Daddy needed him to. He was stubborn but versatile and sure-footed. I rode on the back and held on tightly to Wendy. I couldn't have been happier doing anything in the world than heading up to Slim and Beatrice's camp with Daddy leading the way. I glanced off to the side hills and spotted Sam watching my herd. He waved a big wave as we were getting started. It made me happy that all was well with him. At least I hoped it was. Then my mind turned back to our trail ride.

Daddy led the way. Jim was next, then Wendy and I. Charlie was good about following when he was on a trail ride. Fortunately he saved his stubbornness for when one of us was riding him at home and he didn't want to go somewhere. He just plain didn't go. We wound up the trail which got narrower and narrower the higher we went. The bottom of the canyon blazed with summer flowers. The sound of birds and squirrels was all around us. The fragrance of pine and sage was pungent and wonderful.

As we meandered along, Daddy pointed out different things to us. Eventually we reached a fence with an arched gate and a sign: "National Forest Land." Jim held Daddy's horse while he opened the gate. We rode through and then Daddy secured the gate behind us. He mounted up and we journeyed on. We were about at the end point off Daddy's private land and onto government land. Daddy had a permit to graze a certain number of sheep there for the summer. Other ranchers did the same in various other U.S. forests.

It felt chilly in the shade of the pines as the trail got narrower and more closed in. But Daddy told us to bring jackets, so we put them on. He was so wise and always knew about the weather and what to expect. We could hear the click and scraping sound of the horses' shoes on the rocks as we went through a patch of rough, rocky terrain. Eventually the trail widened out again and there weren't as many rocks. To my surprise the trail led into an opening, a high pasture-like area.

There on the edge of it was a large canvas tent in the sunshine and three or four hobbled horses grazing nearby. A gray-haired woman sat on a tree stump near the tent door with her back to us. Two sleepy border collies lay at her feet. The dogs jumped up and growled as we approached and Daddy dismounted. The dogs sniffed at Daddy's legs but decided he wasn't a threat and went back to stretch out in the sun.

I knew the woman was Beatrice. She heard the dogs and the sound of horses and turned to face us. As she stood, she smiled and yelled, "Hey, Honey Slim! Hey, Honey Slim!" Slim emerged from the tent with a wide smile. They walked forward together to greet us. We dismounted and held the horses so they wouldn't get spooked. Beatrice always called her mate Honey Slim, which made Daddy smile, partly because he was pleased to see her and maybe partly because Beatrice had no teeth. She had bright hazel eyes and was darkly tanned with a slender figure. At one time she probably was an attractive woman, but I guessed her to be older than Mama. My young mind could never tell for sure how old adults were.

Slim was a handsome, middle-aged man with slick black hair and a broad smile. Since he spoke little English, Beatrice was his interpreter and obvious soul mate. If I was older I might have wondered what brought them to this point in their lives and how they ever got to our place in rural southeastern Idaho. But I was more interested in the quaintness of the setting. I thought of Sam and his pretty wife with the fancy car and her broad-brimmed hat. Both Sam and Slim were sheepherders, but their wives and lifestyles seemed so different.

We tied our horses and Charlie to the bushes where they could nibble and walked over to the tent. There was still enough moisture from the morning dew that the distinct smell of the canvas was strong. But the sun was warming things up fast. We took off our jackets and tied them behind our saddles.

Daddy and Slim sat on a large log near the tent to discuss sheep business. Daddy pulled a folded map from his pocket and they studied it together with Beatrice. It showed the boundaries of the government grazing agreement and things like that. It was important for Slim to understand clearly where the sheep could be and where they could not be. Breaking regulations could bring big fines.

They also discussed losing sheep to coyotes, especially big healthy lambs. In one night coyotes could kill as many as eight or ten lambs. They didn't really eat them, just killed one for sport and then went after another. The law of the jungle was sometimes hard for us kids to accept or understand. We heard many conversations about how devastating the losses could be. Ranchers were frustrated that only a designated government trapper could eliminate a predator. It was unlawful for a rancher to shoot or kill a coyote even to protect his own herd. Sometimes I wondered who made the rules.

Sheep rested in the shade during the heat of the day and the coyotes didn't bother them. But in the evening while the sheep were grazing, or late in the dark hours of the night, the coyotes ruled the forest and took their prey. I was glad my herder Sam kept good watch over my herd back at the mouth of the canyon. Daddy's herd was much, much larger than mine.

Daddy told us to mount up since we were going up to the water hole and salt troughs. Slim and Beatrice took the hobbles off a couple of their horses and saddled them to go with us. I was in awe of Beatrice as she flung her heavy saddle onto the horse's back with ease. Her small frame was deceiving. The dogs jumped up, ready for adventure, but Slim commanded them to "stay." They lay back down in the sun like lifeless pelts at his command.

We were starting to feel the heat and the horse flies buzzed around us as we left the clearing single file. Slim led, then Daddy. Beatrice was next, then us kids, doubled up on Charlie, were the last of the string. Although the trails were narrow, there seemed to be lots of grass everywhere on the forest floor. I could smell the unmistakable scent of sheep. It was the lanolin in their wool that threw off the odor. To those who don't like sheep it is unpleasant, but to those of us who ate our bread and butter and wore shoes because of the sheep, it was not unpleasant. It was in our souls just like the scent of raw petroleum is familiar near oil refineries.

It wasn't long before we could see sheep lying in the shade of the pines and mahogany trees and low brush on the hillsides.

They chewed their cuds and watched us cautiously. But sheep know their shepherds. They knew Slim and Beatrice and they knew Daddy, though they must have wondered who we straggly kids were.

We paused while Daddy looked them over. Seeming pleased, he continued on. About ten minutes later we came to the water hole. There was a pipe that came up out of the ground and bent in an L-shape. It dripped its tiny stream of water into a huge metal trough. The pipe was supported with wooden posts. Not many feet away was a place with no grass, a rather drab looking spot where three long low troughs lay. They were obviously the salt troughs which were filled from time to time with rock salt for the sheep. The ground around the troughs was a whitish color. I'm not sure how the big water trough got packed into the area, but more than once I heard Daddy and other men talk about taking salt up to the sheep on pack horses.

My mind turned to Sam and my own herd. I was sure he was careful to give them water and salt too. In fact I thought of Sam often and was glad he was never far away.

Daddy checked to make sure the water was flowing okay, the sheep were content, and all was well with Slim and Beatrice. He gave them the map and bade them farewell. He led as we began wending our way back down the canyon. About thirty minutes later he stopped in a grassy place and told us to dismount, it was time for lunch.

Mama had packed us lunch which was in the saddle bags. There were slices of homemade bread which were already buttered, some canned Vienna sausages and lots of homemade cookies. Of course we carried canteens on our saddles, so we always had fresh water to drink. We sat for a few minutes while the horses grazed on the grass. Canned sausages were low on my list of favorite things, but they tasted good that day in the canyon air, especially with bread and butter wrapped around them. Our lunch stop was short and we were on our way again.

We had no sooner mounted and started down the trail when we met a man coming up. He wore a blue plaid shirt and looked like the lumberjack in a picture book Mama had read to me. I held tightly to Wendy's waist. Daddy stopped and exchanged greetings. He said his name was Norman Schupe, a government trapper, who had been there a few days setting traps for coyotes.

Daddy was polite, but I could tell he wasn't his usual relaxed, cordial self. The man went on up the trail and we continued down. If he was really a trapper, why didn't he have a government jacket or insignia or something on him? Why was he afoot? And why was he trapping way below the government boundary line? I wondered if Sam saw him when he was lower in the canyon.

*Evie at play with little brother.*

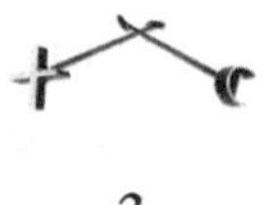

## 3

## HOME SWEET HOME

We got home late in the afternoon rather trail-weary. When we pulled into the barnyard we each helped unsaddle the horses, or in our case, mule. Daddy helped us because we weren't very old. But we were taught to help as much as we could. The two horses and Charlie the mule were anxious to get to the water trough by the barn. They gulped and sucked, and as they raised their heads water streamed from their mouths. We led them to the corral gate behind the barn and took off their bridles.

Charlie liked to lie down in front of the gate and roll over a few times in the dirt. After rolling he always stood and shook his whole body until the dust and dirt collected from the day went flying out around him. We all jumped back and covered our faces with our hands. That was his finale.

We squealed with delight whenever he rolled over. Daddy said when he made it all the way over he was worth a hundred dollars. So we watched and counted to see how much he was worth each time. On this day he only rolled a couple of times because he was in a hurry to get to the rich green grass in the pasture behind the barn. He had had a big day, as we all had. Then Daddy opened the pole gate to the pasture and we took the bridles off. The four-legged threesome trotted happily into their home-sweet-home pasture.

We shook off our dusty clothes and hung our jackets in the back room before entering the kitchen, then we scrambled to see who got to the bathroom first. We could smell something wonderful cooking in the oven. It would be a perfect way to end a long day. But first Daddy and my brother Jim went to the barn to milk the cows. Daddy kept two or three that needed to be milked during the summer. Usually he and Jim could milk them in the time it took some of the rest of us to feed the pet lambs and chickens and lock the chickens in for the night so skunks and weasels wouldn't get them.

After chores I sat on the back porch in an old wicker chair that was there for as long as I could remember. The quietness of the early evening started to unfold, when animals low rather than bellow. Sam walked in from the barnyard and sat on the edge of the wooden porch near my chair. I was glad to have a chance to talk to him alone. The last two days were wonderful but busy. I was worried about the coyotes but he assured me that if my herd was down low in the canyon it would be okay. He told me I was a good girl and he was glad to work for me.

He was concerned about the man in the blue shirt too, because he walked right past Sam, rather close, and didn't stop to talk. I told him Daddy had spoken with him and his name was Norman Schupe, a government trapper. Sam raised his eyebrow and chewed on a straw in his teeth. He had to get home to Mary but said he would be back before sun-up tomorrow to check on my herd. Mama called us all to supper. I left the wicker chair, then turned to tell Sam goodbye, but he was already gone.

At supper Daddy told Mama about our trail ride and reported on other events of the day. Wendy, Jim and I listened with approval, having been there to see it all first-hand. The big girls listened but were glad they didn't have to be in the dust and hot sun like we were. At their adolescent age they deemed themselves too sophisticated to do such things. Wendy and I looked at each other and rolled our eyes. And the little kids, well, they just thought all of life was an adventure and argued about things in their own small world.

Daddy seemed concerned as he told about the man in the blue shirt. Mama said someone came by in the afternoon looking for Daddy. He wore a green jacket with a government insignia. She gave him directions to Sage Canyon but didn't watch which way he went.

While we were at the table Jim asked Daddy if he could have one of the pet lambs for a summer 4-H project. He had just turned ten, the required age to join a club and have a project. Daddy agreed and the next morning he would help Jim pick out one of the best lambs and make arrangements with the club leader. Jim was all smiles.

We finished eating and everyone helped clean up the dishes and kitchen. Mama put the three boys, Mason, Mack and Little Larry, in the bathtub together. It was a good time to catch those three wild boys and scrub them clean. They shared bathwater because hot water was at a premium. The water was heated by the wood-fired cook stove. Right after supper there was enough hot water for dishes and maybe two baths.

Sometimes after supper Mama turned the radio on and we listened to music while we read or played board games on the living room linoleum. There was a big round braided rug in the middle of the floor which made the living room warmer in the winter. In the summer we often didn't need the heat, but it was still a cozy place to be.

Daddy sat in his chair reading by the lamp. Mama often mended clothes by hand or with her Singer sewing machine. Ginny, Nancy and I liked to draw pictures or color. The little boys seemed to have extra energy after their bath so they zoomed around until Daddy made them calm down. The big girls would be talking about friends, movies or magazines. Wendy and Jim might be collaborating on something they were working on. The important thing is we were all together.

As the radio music filtered through the room it had a calming influence on my soul. Hearts can just soak in the soothing sounds. One song that especially stuck in my memory was "...be it ever so humble, there's no place like home." Truly we owned a little bit of heaven. Sleep came easy after our big trail ride.

A new day dawned. Lambs needed to be fed, cows milked, and the chickens let into the protective-wire chicken run. Mama was busy in the kitchen. Jim and Daddy did the chores while Wendy and I and the big girls helped Mama get breakfast on the table. Today's menu included eggs, toast and oatmeal. Our morning prayer was said with most of us kneeling by our chairs. The moment we heard "amen" we scrambled to turn them around and climb up to eat. The younger kids shared a long bench along the wall on one side of the table and could sit for the prayer.

Daddy and Jim went to pick a lamb for his 4-H project. He told the rest of us to help Mama get the garden plot ready to plant. Each year she raised a big vegetable garden in a little area just off the grassy yard. Daddy would plow and disc it. Then we took rakes and tediously combed through all the soil, breaking up lumps and leveling in preparation for planting. It was always fun for the first fifteen minutes. The next several hours were not so fun.

The lamb Jim chose was the biggest one in the pen of pet lambs. He was aggressive and eager to eat. Daddy made a halter-like thing to put on his face and shoulders so they could control him outside the pen. He was to be officially weighed at the beginning of the project. Then a daily record of his food intake would be kept, with more weigh-ins at certain intervals during the next ten weeks until the county fair.

Jim named him Monroe, which sounded regal to me. He was instantly in love with Monroe. Jim kept him apart from the other lambs since they were having milk a little longer as some of them were born quite runty. Monroe, a little older, progressed to other feed such as dry hay leaves, lamb pellets and green grass. Too much grass could cause indigestion so he had to be monitored. Jim was delighted to oblige. Monroe was lucky to have a boy like Jim to protect and take care of him.

The next several days felt good. We planted the garden and Jim spent lots of time with Monroe. We all reveled in the blossoming of summer. Yellow dandelions were everywhere. I talked to Sam whenever he came around. Sometimes it was several times a day. But then I might go for a few days without seeing him at all. He was on my mind a lot and I wondered if he had children our age. He never mentioned children. His most important role was to be there for my herd—and for me. It seemed like whenever I was sad or worried or lonely he was suddenly there, smiling, always chewing on a stem of hay or grass.

Daddy and the other adults smiled at my imaginary sheepherder, but Sam was real to me. I found comfort in knowing he would be there whenever I needed him.

Monroe grew like a weed. He became so gentle he tried to follow Jim wherever he went. As healthy lambs do, Monroe soon took on a flat, square-back look. Many pet lambs end up with a fat belly but a spiny back bone caused by fewer feedings. But not Monroe. He was picture-perfect.

The next week Daddy suggested we do a cook-out up the canyon for supper one night. We jumped up and down with excitement. We did our work all that day and helped Mama get the food and things ready to take to the canyon. I thought we would go to Sage Canyon as we usually did, but when it was almost time to go Daddy said we were going to Smith Canyon, a mile or so farther north of Sage Canyon. Daddy wanted to go there so he could talk to a rancher at the mouth of Smith Canyon.

We piled in the truck with all the things Mama prepared. There were a couple of boxes with food and a wire picnic basket with all the utensils. Daddy also put in a large folded canvas and two cast-iron Dutch ovens. Mama and Little Larry rode in the cab with Daddy. The rest of us, even the big girls, rode in the back. We sang and laughed and had such fun riding along. It was bumpy and dusty, but nonetheless glorious. The anticipation of a cook-out and just being together with Mama and Daddy and the whole family lent a feeling of completeness seldom equaled.

Daddy stopped at the ranch house by Smith Canyon so he could talk to the man. We all waited in the truck like obedient dogs who were told to *stay*. Daddy took off his hat when the man came to the door and held it as they talked. We were too far away to hear the conversation. They finished their powwow and shook hands. Daddy put his hat on and strode back to the truck.

We continued through a gate and then along a rutty dirt road through the trees until we came to a shallow stream. There was a grassy opening where Daddy parked the truck. We all climbed out. Daddy spread the canvas out so Mama could set up her supper preparations. He gathered some rocks and wood and soon had a hot fire burning. I loved the smell of the pine wood burning and the crack of the fire. Mama let us wade as long as we did not get our clothes wet. The rocks in the creek were brown and mineral colored and the water made a soothing sound as it bubbled over and around them. It was paradise. Before long we could smell the food cooking in the Dutch ovens. We were having such fun playing in and near the creek. It was like a fairyland come true.

Just when Mama told the big girls to come and help, Lucy let out a scream that seemed to pierce the entire canyon. A crawdad had grabbed her toe and was clinging on with its powerful pincers. Daddy came running and pulled it off and carried Lucy back to the picnic area. She was sobbing as a trickle of blood ran across her big toe and seeped between the other toes. Mama tied a strip of cloth around her toe and tried to comfort her. We all were horrified, especially the boys, but were also enthralled with the idea of something creepy lying in wait to grab us in that seemingly gentle brook. After that we waded more gingerly as we played.

I sat by Lucy on the canvas and put my shoes back on. I could hear Daddy and Mama as they continued a conversation they were having before the crawdaddy attack. Daddy was telling Mama that the man he had just seen told him the bank was robbed in a place called Rock Springs, Wyoming a few days ago. There were three robbers. The police caught two of them, but one got away and still had the stolen money. The man told Daddy the robbers got away with twenty thousand dollars. That was a number too big for me to figure in my mind, but I knew it was huge when Daddy whistled as he repeated the amount. Rock Springs was more than a hundred miles away, said Daddy.

A shiver ran up my spine to think a bank robber was somewhere out there. I was glad Rock Springs was a hundred miles away. Again my calculations were skewed by my innocence, but that seemed a good safe distance from our world, and I was glad. Jim, on the other hand, had also been listening and thought of adventure. Nothing exciting like that ever happens around here, he said.

"Don't be so sure," said Daddy. He explained the Montpelier bank itself was once robbed, by one of the most famous outlaws ever. He was known as Butch Cassidy. I had heard of Hopalong Cassidy but not Butch Cassidy. Daddy continued: "About sixty years ago, Butch Cassidy and two members of his gang robbed the Montpelier bank. Cassidy scooped the money into a gunny sack, got on his horse and rode away. The other two outlaws followed on their horses. The deputy sheriff chased them out of town on a big-wheeled bicycle and a posse tracked them for a week. One outlaw was caught but Cassidy and the other outlaw took the money and got clean away."

The smell of supper was heavenly. Daddy lifted the heavy ovens off the fire onto a flat rock with a hooked stick he whittled. We all sat around on the big canvas. Mama placed a checkered tablecloth in the middle. She always made things seem homey and wonderful no matter the setting. Daddy had little Mack, who was only four, say our prayer on the food. Among other things he sweetly asked for Lucy's toe to not get bit anymore. We all agreed with "amen."

Mama filled our plates and we enjoyed a most wonderful meal. There was plenty of time after supper for a little more wading and adventure-seeking through the quaking aspen trees while Mama and Daddy cleaned up. Since Lucy was crippled she got out of her usual big-girl chores. It meant Kari, Wendy and I had to pitch in and help pack things back into the boxes and basket. We rinsed the metal camp plates in the creek, Mama saying we would wash them with hot water and soap when we got home. I couldn't see why, but I was a kid and adults always won on deals like that.

Before Daddy put the fire out and the coals were still glowing, we gathered around and roasted marshmallows on long skinny sticks he whittled. Nothing ever tasted as sweet and yummy as the warm, soft, sugary treat on the end of our sticks. Most of it went in our mouths and some on our cheeks and fingers.

It was a good way to end another perfect day, at least for everyone except Lucy. She sat in the front of the truck with Daddy, Mama, and Little Larry on the way home. We sang and laughed all the way. We didn't care that we all smelled like campfire smoke and had mud and marshmallows stuck to us. We were a family and we were happy.

As we went past the lane that led to Sage Canyon I wondered if Sam was still there or if he had gone home to Mary. It was getting dark so I supposed he had gone home.

*Feeding a "bum" lamb.*

# 4

# DADDY TO THE RESCUE

Next morning after breakfast and chores, Daddy asked who wanted to come along while he took Charlie to Smith Canyon. Wendy and Jim and I all shouted at once that we wanted to be the one. An amused smile spread across Daddy's face. He declared all three of us could go.

Jim would ride Pomp. Wendy and I would ride together on Charlie like the day we went to Slim and Beatrice's camp. The man at Smith Canyon wanted to borrow Charlie for a few days for a pack trip. We were to ride the horse and mule to Smith Canyon and then Daddy would meet us there in the truck and see us back home. It was about a four-mile ride so we needed to get started. Daddy helped us saddle up. He knew Charlie would cooperate better with the other horse coming along.

We visited a little as we went along, but mostly we just enjoyed the freedom and adventure of the moment. I wondered if my herd was still safe. I hadn't seen Sam for a few days. When we neared the Sage Canyon turn off, I searched the hillside with my eyes for what might be a glimpse of him or the sheep, but saw nothing. It seemed I saw him mostly when I was alone for some reason. But it didn't matter. I knew he was taking care of my herd and would report back to me when he could.

We rode for about an hour before reaching the Smith Canyon ranch. Daddy's red truck was coming behind us with perfect timing. The man came out of his house and he and Daddy visited for a few minutes. Daddy took the saddle and bridle off Charlie and put them in the back of the truck. He tied Pomp to the tailgate to trot home. He asked if any of us wanted to ride him home, but we declined. We rode in the back of the truck. Jim sat on the saddle like on a bucking horse and we all laughed. As we pulled out of the man's barnyard and drove away we could hear Charlie braying. I felt sort of bad for leaving him there.

I was thinking maybe the man at Smith Canyon would let Sam keep my herd over there for the rest of the summer. Having seen grassy areas in the canyon on our cook-out the evening before, I could imagine my herd grazing there with dependable, wonderful Sam on his horse watching over them. Yes, that is what I'd have Sam do.

A day or two later when Daddy was asking his usual suppertime questions to each of us, he asked how Sam and my herd were doing. When I told him they were now in Smith Canyon he looked taken aback but knew under the circumstances my herd could be wherever I wanted.

The next week was filled with busy happenings. Monroe continued to gallop behind Jim like a dog. The pet lambs were moved to a small pasture on the north side of the yard. Monroe spent most of his time with them, but the moment he saw Jim come near the fence he leaped and hopped like a deer to get to him. Of course, Jim always had a handful of lamb pellets for him. As part of the 4-H project Jim had to train Monroe to be led by a little halter. The goal was to keep Monroe calm and controlled with no jumping or darting so he could be ready for the lamb show at the county fair in a few weeks. But Monroe didn't have a clue about county fairs. All he wanted was to follow Jim around, hoping for a pellet treat.

Daddy was working in one of his fields not far from Sage Canyon Lane. It was about eighty acres of rocky sagebrush land he purchased a few years earlier for a decent price because it was unworked land.

Sagebrush grew wild and tall and was deep-rooted. Daddy rented a piece of farm equipment called a sagebrush beater and hooked it behind his small, gray Ford tractor. It caught the sagebrush bushes and yanked them up by the roots as it passed over them. Then it would mangle and roll them out the back, leaving a trail of deadwood debris behind. It was an imperfect way to deal with the bushes but so much better than digging them out by hand as his forefathers did.

The next step was to gather the sagebrush rubble and heap it into piles to be burned. That's where we came in. Daddy divided us into two groups with three kids in each. One of the big girls was in charge. Then there was a middle kid and a younger kid. The youngest ones weren't assigned. They roamed at will and helped where they wanted. Kari, Jim and I were one group. The other group had Lucy, Wendy and Ginny. We carried armfuls of brush to a pile until our leader Kari deemed it high enough. Then we moved to another area and began the process again until we had several tall piles ready to burn.

Daddy gave each group a spray can with coal oil in it. It was the type of can we used to spray cow flies off the milk cows in the summer. There was a little can-like tank on one end and a cylinder with a plunger in it on the other end. When the plunger was pushed, it forced air through and the fluid sprayed out of a little hole on the end of the can. We were to spray the coal oil into one small area at the bottom of the sage pile. Then we were to stand back as the team leader lit a match to it. The rest of the pile would soon become inflamed and the pile would burn.

We wore long-sleeved shirts even though it was a hot summer day. We wore brown jersey gloves to protect our hands from the rough, slivery branches of the sage. Most of us wore some kind of head covering as well. Kari and Lucy wore bandannas of course to match their other clothing. I had on my favorite blue felt hat I wore almost everywhere outdoors. I guess at seven years old I wasn't concerned about fashion or fad, just practical use.

Daddy came across the field on the tractor to tell us to light the fires before the wind whipped up as it usually did toward afternoon. Then he went back across the field to continue his work. Kari sprayed and then lit the first pile. In a few seconds it was a huge blaze with the unmistakable odor of burning sage as smoke billowed from it.

We moved to the second pile. Kari sprayed and set the can down near the pile while striking the match. It ignited and immediately the flame leaped to the spray can. We were horrified. Kari demanded I give her my blue hat to smother the flame on the oil can. I would not. She insisted. I still would not. We all backed away from the blazing can. Kari grabbed my hat and bravely used it to try to smother the fire on the can. It didn't work because the can was too engulfed. My blue hat was ruined. It was full of blackened burn holes and I was devastated. I started to cry. Everyone gathered around to see my hat. Kari explained she was trying to save us because she thought the can would explode and kill us all. By then Daddy saw the commotion and came across the field to where we were standing. I was howling and the tears ran down my dirty face.

He rushed over and got on his knees in front of me while we told our story. He took the big, ever-present red handkerchief from his back pocket and wiped my cheeks. Then he picked me up, something that didn't happen often anymore because there were so many others younger than I. He carried me to the red truck parked near the gate. He sat me on the shady side of the seat and had me drink cold water from the canvas water bag he always carried in the truck.

He called me a brave and good girl for letting them use my hat to protect everyone. He flipped the scenario around in my mind so that I was the hero instead of the wimpy, picked-on kid who was too selfish to help in a crisis. He told me to rest there for a few minutes before I helped with the brush again.

Daddy went back and talked to the others. I don't know what he said, but as always he spread a balm of kindness over us that made us want to be kind to each other and be helpful where we could. Of course the hat was finished. I felt bad about it because I really loved it. But it didn't hurt as much or seem as important after Daddy talked to me. I took it home to show Mama and then it disappeared.

Before heading home Daddy drove to our cabin to make sure everything was okay. When we reached the cabin I was about to cross the threshold when something caught my eye. I reached down and picked up a blue button. How could it have gotten there? The other kids gathered pine cones, rocks and other natural objects, but I figured I had the most interesting treasure, the mysterious blue button.

I was hoping to see Sam that evening so I could tell him about my hat. Sure enough after supper when things were quiet he was standing in the backyard. I related my tale and he patted me on the head and said maybe I could get a new hat and I'd be okay. My sheep were doing really well after being herded to Smith Canyon and he liked it over there. I knew things would be okay and went in the house to be with my family.

*Brother and Evie taking a fishing break.*

# 5

# CRIME AND JUSTICE

Our evening baths were especially soothing after the dusty, smoky, tiring day we all spent in the sagebrush field. Calm came over me as I lay on my stomach on the braided rug in the living room, drawing pictures and listening to music on the old brown radio. Daddy was reading and Mama humming to the music as she mended clothes.

Wendy suffered with a bad sore throat for a few weeks. She had been sick in the winter also. When she was feeling better the doctor said she should have her tonsils out and would have to stay overnight at the hospital. The big day came and Daddy and Mama took her to town for the surgery.

We were told what to do while they were gone, but we were distracted and half-hearted about our work. Jim got the brilliant idea that he and I could skip away unnoticed and do some fishing along the creek that ran east of our place up to the foothills. Our poles were willows with a little fish line wound around them and a hook tied on the end. Creek fishing was iffy at best. It was more an adventure than a real fishing trip. But the thought of getting away was exhilarating to me. I was honored for Jim to take me along. Usually he and Wendy were cohorts since they were closer in age. But with her headed to surgery I was the chosen one.

We followed the creek through endless willows. In a place or two where the creek widened we could actually see a few small trout in the water but we lacked the finesse to interest them in our poor bait which was a couple of skinny earthworms. We came across a dead Hereford bull lying in tall pasture grass. The stench was overwhelming. We saw maggots crawling around on it. Jim thought they would make good bait, but the odor was so intense and gagging he couldn't get close enough to get one. I was not getting near something so repulsive.

The creek meandered down as we meandered up. After spending hours drowning worms, we got skunked and gave up. By now the sun had moved quite a way in the sky and Jim and I headed back. Going home took a while as we worked our way through the willows again. But we were still thrilled about our daring adventure.

To our horror, however, when we finally got home we saw that Daddy and Mama had beat us there and our little escapade was discovered. It was already suppertime. We were punished for going away for the whole day without permission. I had to scrub the bathroom and Jim milked all three cows alone without help. We didn't have electric milkers and Daddy was particular about the cows being completely milked out. No cutting corners. Meanwhile I scrubbed the tub and sink with cleanser. I cleaned the toilet with some green powder and a brush. Then I got on my knees and mopped the floor with a rag and Lysol water Mama fixed for me. I felt picked on. But I felt worse for Jim. Bad as my punishment was, his was worse. And we weren't allowed to speak to each other the rest of the evening.

The next morning Mama drove Wendy to the hospital and brought her home. She looked pale but smiled bravely as she walked into the house with a balloon on the end of a little stick. Mama put her right to bed. She was to rest for a few days. Her voice was creaky so she mostly just nodded or smiled. Mama put a little brass bell on a chair by her bed so if she needed something she could ring it and someone would come running.

That night Mama came into the girls' bedroom to tell us goodnight. To say her own evening prayer, she knelt by Wendy's bed. We all felt warmed by the gesture. Then Ginny asked if Mama would say her prayer by *her* bed the next night. And so it went after that. We would ask for Mama to pray by our beds. Sometimes the asking began early in the day at breakfast time. Soon the boys caught on and wanted Mama to pray by their beds too. That tradition carried on for several years. What comfort a prayerful mother can be.

Jim and I didn't dare think of fishing again for weeks. But we had the memory of an exhilarating adventure that still plays on my mind sometimes on a summer day.

We continued clearing the sagebrush field an acre at a time. Daddy thanked us for doing a good job and clearing ten acres. The next step was to haul rocks off before he could plow. He hooked the hay rack to the back of the little gray tractor. We gathered rocks and put them on the hayrack. Then Daddy would drive forward a little and we'd clear rocks from new sections. So it went, over and over.

Each time the hayrack was full he drove it to a corner of the field. We all climbed aboard and began throwing rocks into a big pile. The process was repeated many times. Some of the rocks were so big it was all Daddy could do to lift them or pry them out of the dirt with his shovel. His goal was to get the ten acres cleared and tilled before the summer was over. The following year he would work on another ten acres.

*Daddy's cabin was built in 1932.*

# 6

# SURPRISE VISITORS

Often in the evening just before the sun went down we played in the yard after supper. It was amazing we had any energy left. Sam often came by and talked to me in the backyard when I was alone. It was good he came often because it made me feel secure to know he was there and my herd was safe. He said my lambs were getting bigger each day and still loved being in Smith Canyon.

Wendy recovered soon. She was supposed to take it easy for a few days so she read a book or two. In the 1950s we had no television to watch. Few people had them. At our house there was never time to be bored or lonesome, however, because there were always people around.

The man from Smith Canyon came by with Charlie tied behind his truck. He was safe after being used for a pack trip of some kind. Charlie was happy to be home and displayed it by rolling over four times in the dirt. That was worth four hundred dollars! Then he shivered and shook vigorously, as the dust and debris flew off him and covered all of us. He brayed with obvious pleasure as we led him into his pasture. His bray this time was a call of joy at being home again.

Daddy learned the bank robber who got away was still missing. The Rock Springs police hired a detective to try to find him. The detective went as far away as Colorado and Utah talking to people. I was glad we lived in Idaho.

Jim continued to spend lots of time with Monroe. He tied his halter to a post of Mama's clothesline in the backyard. Then he took a bucket of water and cleaned and brushed Monroe's short, curly wool within an inch of his life. Monroe didn't mind any of Jim's antics as long as he was allowed to nibble the green grass and be close to Jim. They were inseparable and Monroe was growing bigger and stronger.

After Charlie was home a couple of days, Daddy needed to take some supplies to Slim and Beatrice's camp. It was too soon for Wendy to make the hard ride. Jim had an important 4-H Club demonstration to give and he couldn't miss it or he would forfeit. The big girls were busy, didn't like riding horses per se, and were Mama's best helpers, so they didn't want to make the trip. I was hoping Daddy would want me to go with him. But his decision was to drive the truck to his cabin as usual and then ride Sundance, leading Charlie loaded with the pack of supplies. He planned to go the next morning.

Daddy first needed to go to Montpelier, five miles away, to get the supplies. He let Wendy ride in the truck for a little outing and, joy of joys, I got to go too! Mama made fresh braids for both of us. We stopped at the feed store and got some lamb pellets for Monroe. Daddy also got four sacks of rock salt to take to Slim. Then we went to the grocery store where he loaded up on lots of food staples like flour, sugar, a slab of bacon, canned milk, and wheat and oatmeal cereals. It was so fun to ride along in the cab of the truck.

Daddy stopped at a service station and a man with a rag in his back pocket came and put a gas hose into the truck. He washed the dirty windshield and put the hood up and did some things under there. While he was doing that, Daddy went inside the little station and came out with three root beers in little glass bottles. He popped the lids off. It was like Christmas in the summer to have a treat like that! We sipped and drank and burped a little to each other while Daddy talked to the man. We finished our drinks and Daddy took the bottles back into the store since they had to be returned. He paid for the gas and root beer and we headed for home. It seemed like every day that summer was filled with excitement and adventure.

As dawn broke the next morning, Daddy loaded the huge white canvas pack saddles with the items he was taking up the canyon. He loaded it all in the back of the truck, saddled Sundance, and put the pack frame on Charlie. He tied them to the back of the truck and left, saying he would be home before dark. Actually it was way after dark. Mama was worried sick and kept looking out the kitchen window for his headlights to come into the barnyard. When he finally got home the little kids had gone to bed but the rest of us gathered around the kitchen table as Daddy, tired as could be, unlaced his high boots and told the story of his day.

When Daddy got to the bottom of Sage Canyon that morning he could see a thin stream of smoke wafting up through the pine trees and rising into the early morning light just before dawn. At first he feared the start of a forest fire. But as he approached his cabin he could see the smoke was coming out of the chimney. There was an older model truck parked nose-first near the cabin door. It was surprising to say the least. Although it was long before sunrise, he went to the door and knocked. Our truck made noise coming up the road, so it should not have been a surprise to whoever was inside when he knocked.

A man who Daddy guessed to be in his fifties answered the door with his trousers on and his suspenders over his white undershirt. He lit a lantern since there was no electricity and the morning was still mostly shadows. Daddy explained he owned the cabin and asked the stranger who he was. He said he and his wife were traveling across the country from Oklahoma to Oregon in search of work and decided to find a place to camp for a few days.

They explored two or three local canyons. When they found Daddy's cabin and saw it was deserted, they decided to stay a while. He said he was a scissor salesman but since the war he hadn't done well at it. They had relatives in Oregon and were headed there in hopes their kinfolk would put them up until he found work.

About that time a woman got up out of bed and also came to the door. They invited Daddy to step in. Well, it seemed strange to me that Daddy needed an invitation to step into his own cabin. Nonetheless, he stepped in. They must have been there for several days because it looked lived in. They were soft-spoken and apologetic, not at all threatening. Daddy was skeptical when the guy said he was a scissors salesman, until he opened two suitcase-like chests, filled with all kinds of scissors.

Daddy, kind-hearted by nature, told the couple they could stay for a few more days, then they needed to move along. They thanked him for being understanding. He told them he would be coming and going through there quite a bit and cautioned them to be careful with fire in the forested area.

We were wide-eyed at the thought of a strange couple living in the cabin. Daddy continued his tale of the day. He loaded the saddle bag packs on Charlie and led him behind Sundance as he went up the long trail to Slim and Beatrice's camp. Having been there three weeks earlier, Jim, Wendy and I were reliving our own trail ride as Daddy told the story. I could almost hear the birds and smell the pine and sage as he talked. He traveled slowly with the pack load, thinking Charlie was still worn out from the trip with the man from Smith Canyon, so they stopped several times to rest.

When Daddy got to Slim and Beatrice's camp he was welcomed as always. Slim helped unload the supplies. Beatrice was preparing breakfast as he arrived so the three of them ate and visited, with Beatrice doing most of the interpreting and talking. Slim said the sheep were doing well and the coyotes killed fewer sheep since the government trapper arrived. I was especially interested in what he had to say about the trapper because I still thought there was something mysterious about him. And the blue button was still tucked away in my dresser drawer.

Daddy laughed when he described eating breakfast with Slim and Beatrice, who had no teeth. It made us all laugh a little. Then he got serious again. Slim had ridden across to the north just out of Daddy's grazing allotment to check for sheep a few days ago. He was making sure no strays had wandered off, which is what a good sheep herder does.

Slim had come across a huge rattlesnake, whose rattle terrified his horse, which stomped and bucked, nearly throwing Slim. Saved by his savvy horsemanship, Slim then killed the rattler with the pistol he always carried. It was unusual for a rattlesnake to be in that area. Mostly they were a few miles farther north where the pines met the cedars and where there were lots of old volcanic rock beds. They had not previously been seen near the local canyons.

A shiver ran down my back as Daddy talked about the snake. Slim stretched it out and it was well over five feet long. He held up the line of rattles for Daddy to inspect.

*Eve with siblings and friends on four legs.*

## 7

## HORSE SENSE

Then came the sad part of the story. Daddy strapped the empty pack saddle bags back onto Charlie and mounted Sundance. He bade farewell to Slim and Beatrice, saying he would check on them again in a couple of weeks and bring more supplies. He started winding his way down the canyon. Sundance was reluctant to move along. Daddy kept urging him and Sundance would go a short way and then stop to rest. Suddenly he could tell Sundance was getting wobbly so he got off and led him quite a ways. The reins tightened in Daddy's hand as Sundance dropped, knees first and then altogether to the ground. He let out a few big sighs, almost grunts, and was dead.

It was unbelievable! We started crying as Daddy told us about it. There were tears in Daddy's eyes too. It had been a terribly upsetting day for him. He was still a long way from the cabin. He took the saddle and bridle off and put them on Charlie's back to carry. Then Daddy, disheartened, led Charlie the rest of the way down the canyon. He knew he could ride but needed to walk so he could think clearly.

There was an old pit-like area not far from where Sundance died. The next day Daddy would go back with two horses and drag Sundance to the pit and cover him up the best he could as a grave. If it had happened off the trail he might have left him there for nature to take care of, but because it was on the trail the horse needed to be moved. Our daddy looked so tired. It was a good thing he hadn't taken a crew of us kids along on that ride. Mama was glad Daddy had the good sense to get off the horse before it fell. Otherwise the fall might have broken his leg.

Sleep didn't come easy that night. There was so much to digest with the thought of people moving into the cabin, Slim killing a huge rattlesnake and, worst of all, Sundance dying. I think we all tossed and turned a lot before sleep found us. I particularly felt sad for Daddy because I knew how much he loved that little golden palomino pony.

The next day Daddy took Pomp and Charlie back to Sage Canyon to take care of the matter with Sundance. He went alone. None of us really wanted to go anyway. While there he visited again with the man and woman in the cabin. Their names were John and Dora Leewood. He enjoyed talking to them about all the places they traveled through. They were interested in the farm and the sheep and the things Daddy was doing. They laughed and couldn't imagine being a family with ten children.

They hadn't been blessed with kids and regretted it. Daddy smelled food cooking and he thought it seemed nice to see the cabin used and appreciated again. But he made no mistake about the fact he wanted them gone before they took up permanent residency.

We were all a little blue that week after losing Sundance. Daddy had us help him haul rocks a few more times and the garden had come up along with long weeds. That meant we had to help pull the weeds on the day after Mama watered it. One day a week it was our turn to have the irrigation water from the creek come through our place. The back pasture got watered by flooding it out across the ground. Then for a couple of hours the water was channeled along a little ditch that led into the garden. Between the row of vegetables was a water row or a small groove dug in the soil to let the water flow slowly through, soaking the plants. Then by the next day it wasn't muddy anymore, just damp and a good time to pull weeds.

Later that week Kari and Luci went to 4-H camp, which had been planned for many weeks. It cost them each ten dollars. I heard Mama and Daddy talking about whether they could afford to send them both at the same time. But they decided the two should go together. The girls were excited as they rolled blankets to make bedrolls tied with a rope and each packed a small bag of clothes.

Mama drove them to town where they met a group of other youths and loaded onto a rented school bus headed for their adventure. The camp was held somewhere on the border of Idaho and Wyoming. I shuddered as I thought about the bank robber being loose in Wyoming. In my little girl mind I could conjure up all kinds of thoughts about the fugitive hiding in the trees at their camp and things like that. But that was the last thing they were thinking as they rode off with friends for an exciting time.

With the big girls gone it left more work for Wendy and me for a few days. But it was so good to have Wendy feeling well again and I truly loved being with her. She and I talked about the rattlesnake as we pulled weeds and hauled rocks. We agreed it was a spooky, terrible thing. We wondered if we would ever get to see the rattles Slim cut off the snake and showed to Daddy.

I wanted to talk to Sam about the snake when I saw him again. He needed to know maybe a snake could come as far south as Smith Canyon. I was hoping I would see him again soon. As we were hauling rocks, I looked over toward Smith

Canyon as I often did, just wondering about my herd, the coyotes and now the possibility of a rattlesnake. Although I didn't see Sam that evening, I knew he must be busy and he would come and talk to me whenever he could. I wanted to tell him about Sundance and so many other things that weighed heavily on my young mind.

I thought about Sam's wife, Mary, and how she was such a lady she would probably scream and lose her hat if she saw a snake. I compared her to how Beatrice probably took it in stride and helped her Honey Slim cut off the rattles. There was such a difference between the two women.

After Sundance died Daddy needed another horse he could use for the trail rides and work around the farm. We had a team he used in the winter to pull the sleigh to feed the sheep. The team was mismatched at best. One was a red sorrel work horse named Red Wing and one was a black horse with a wide white strip down his nose that Daddy named Old Baldy.

To me a horse was a horse, but Daddy pointed out the work horses have thick, heavy legs and big feet while the riding horses have thinner legs and feet. The team didn't always have shoes. Daddy kept their feet trimmed, but since most of their work was done in the winter and they grazed most of the summer and weren't in the rocks, he let them go without shoes. Horse shoes cost money, something we didn't have much of at our house.

Daddy decided to shoe Red Wing. He went into the pasture and brought him to the barnyard with a halter. Red Wing was a little surprised but came along okay. When Old Baldy saw Red Wing being led away, he wanted to come also, but Daddy shut the gate on him and he could only watch curiously through the poles of the gate.

Daddy led Red Wing around the barnyard two or three times to get him acclimated to his setting and get the wiggles out. Then he tied him to the post near the shed where the tools and tack were kept. He told Jim, Wendy and me to stand way back. He knew something simple could turn into a rodeo in an instant if it spooked the horse.

He had his tools and four new horse shoes sitting on a wooden crate next to the post. We watched as he lifted the horse's legs up, one at a time, and trimmed them with big horse-hoof pincers. It was so interesting we didn't even talk to each other. We just gaped. But it was even more unbelievable to watch him actually nail the shoes to the horse's hooves. Daddy held three or four horseshoe nails between his lips so he could quickly reach for one as he needed it. It was amazing he knew where to place the nails without hurting the horse. I was sure Sam could shoe his own horse too.

Now shod, Red Wing was set to be ridden through the rocky terrain to Slim and Beatrice's camp or wherever Daddy decided to take him. For a couple of days Daddy tied him up by the barn with a saddle on his back so he could get used to it since he hadn't been ridden much. Daddy gave him a couple of pitchforks of hay to eat instead of the pasture grass. I wondered if Red Wing knew he had been promoted to a new position.

*Daddy, Mama, with Eve and two siblings ready to ride in the bed of his red truck.*

## 8

## HELPING THE LEEWOODS

Daddy took Mama to town to get glasses. It was the first time she wore glasses and we were all excited to see her when they came home and pulled into the barnyard. We ran out the back door to meet them. I thought she looked pretty, but it was hard to get used to seeing her with them on.

In the evening when she mended clothes or read after supper she often remarked how good it was to see well. When they came home they also brought the big girls with them. They met the group as it returned from 4-H camp. Kari and Lucy were giddy with all they had to tell us younger kids about the things they saw and did during the last four days. Daddy and Mama had bought some groceries and Daddy carried them to the house in a cardboard box. We stood around the table and watched as he took items out of the box and put them on the table.

We cheered when he reached down dramatically and drew out a big Hershey chocolate bar! It was segmented with H-e-r-s-h-e-y on each piece. Daddy carefully broke off a thick segment for each of us. We were thrilled. Some of the kids popped them right into their mouths and began sucking on them. Others were more cautious, cradling the piece in the palm of their hands like a queen's jewel. I nibbled the edge of mine and savored the rich chocolate flavor, then hid it in my drawer next to the blue button. I planned to come back later to the chocolate and to think about the button too.

Daddy planned to go back to Sage Canyon in the morning to check on his "squatters" and the sagebrush field. I didn't know what a squatter was so he explained it was someone who came along and just took over a piece of property without really owning it. I understood then he meant to check his cabin and see if John and Dora Leewood were still there. When the other kids overheard Daddy's plan, they all wanted to go too. Mama agreed, but she needed the big girls to help with the washing. As always we jumped up and down at the thought of going to the canyons.

Daddy wanted to go right after breakfast so we all pitched in to help clean up the dishes and the kitchen. Jim helped Daddy milk the cows before breakfast while Wendy and I fed the chickens. The big girls were good at helping Mama do the clothes washing. It was a big process where metal tubs placed on benches along two sides of the wringer washer were filled with water. In the summer it was done on the big back porch. This time of year it likely helped Mama to have most of us kids out of the way on washday. She probably could have used some help from Wendy and me, but the tom boy in both of us always voted to go on an adventure with Daddy.

Daddy tied Red Wing on behind the truck just to give him a good workout. Most of us rode in the back because we went rather slowly with the horse trotting along behind. Mack and Little Larry were in front with Daddy where he could watch them closer. Wendy, Jim, Ginny, Mason, Nancy and I were the crew in the back. Red Wing didn't seem to like being tied on and balked a little until Daddy got out and patted him and talked to him. He was okay after that. As we approached the canyon areas I looked to the north to see if I might see my herd or Sam anywhere. But I couldn't see anything. We turned and headed up the lane to Sage Canyon. Jim jumped out and opened the gate. Minutes later we were parked in front of Daddy's cabin. The Leewoods' truck was parked there too. One of the back tires was flat. Daddy shut off the motor and told us we could play but stay close. We were like a herd of cats when he turned us loose. We loved to explore and climb up the hill.

He put Mack and little Larry in the back of the truck and told them to play in there and not get out. They seemed okay with it. Wendy and Jim got out and ran up the hill with the other kids, but I stayed in the truck bed with Mack and Little Larry. I wanted to hear what Daddy said to the Leewoods.

He walked up the wooden steps to knock on the door, but it opened almost before he could knock. John Leewood stood there, smiling. They shook hands. Daddy asked how things were going and Mr. Leewood pointed to his old beat-up truck and the flat tire. Mr. Leewood wanted to know if Daddy could take the tire to town to get it fixed because their spare tire was flat too. Being the kind man he is, Daddy offered to take both tires to Montpelier the next time he went.

Mr. Leewood put his hat on and came out to the truck to remove the flat tire. He dug around in the back of his truck until he came up with an old handy-man jack and tire iron. Daddy placed some good-sized rocks behind the other three wheels and helped Mr. Leewood jack up the truck.

When they pried the rusty hubcap off it made a high-pitched screeching sound. Red Wing snorted, jerked his head up and jumped back, pulling the halter lead rope almost to its breaking point. Thankfully, Daddy was able to calm Red Wing down by patting him and talking low to him. I made up my mind right then I wouldn't ever ride Red Wing. I had ridden Old Baldy a time or two, but I didn't plan to ever get on Red Wing's back. He was too giddy and jumpy.

Daddy and Mr. Leewood put the two flat tires in the back of our truck. Mack and Little Larry immediately climbed on them. Daddy walked back to the porch with Mr. Leewood. They talked and shook hands again. Mr. Leewood disappeared inside the cabin as Daddy lifted Mack and Little Larry out and put them in the cab. He whistled and the other kids came running and skidding down the hillside. They climbed in the back of the truck, careful not to get too close to Red Wing. We were all taught to be cautious around a nervous horse.

Then we drove down to the sagebrush field. As we approached we could see the little green sprouts of wheat coming up where we cleared the ten acres of brush and rocks before Daddy tilled and seeded it. It would be a late crop, probably just to graze off in the fall, but by next spring it would become productive. Since the sagebrush field was fairly close to the mouth of Smith Canyon I strained my eyes, as I always did, hoping to see a glimpse of my herd and Sam. I was sure I saw him on his horse on the hillside waving my way. What a comfort that was! Someday I would tell Sam how much security and peace he gave me.

We headed back toward home. As we passed the buttercup field I could see the pretty blossoms were gone. Their spring season of blooming was passed. I didn't want time to pass so fast, but I could see the buttercups were gone, the vegetable garden was getting tall, and Monroe had doubled in size. We were in full-blown summer.

Daddy took the saddle off Red Wing and put him back in the pasture with Old Baldy and the others. Mama and the big girls had laundry hanging on the clothesline and it was sailing slightly in the warm breeze. The washer and tubs were put away. On the living room couch was a mountain of dry laundry to be folded and put away. Some were set aside for ironing.

Mama told Wendy and me to wash our hands and start folding and sorting the clean clothes. Although Ginny and Nancy weren't very old, they could carry the folded piles to a person's bed. Then each family member put their own clothes away in their drawers or closet space. Mama had an efficient system worked out. With ten kids it was a matter of survival.

I heard the clanging of pans in the kitchen as Mama prepared to start supper. It would be an early one because we hadn't eaten since breakfast and the day was fading fast. She fried some chicken and boiled potatoes. It smelled divine. The big girls carried in the last several armloads of dried clothes from the clothesline and heaped them on the couch for us to fold. It seemed like it would take forever. I was thinking I would rather be riding along the hill checking my herd or swinging in the big tire swing Daddy hung on the limb of the crab apple tree—anything but folding laundry. Finally we got it all finished and sat down to eat.

Daddy reported each aspect of our day, including how good the sagebrush field looked because of our hard work. We all felt lots of pride but recalling I had to sacrifice my hat gave me a twinge of pain. Then he told Mama about the two flat tires and that he would have to get them fixed or the Leewoods would never be about to leave. He was sure he would have to pay for the tires himself, because the Leewoods probably didn't have a dime of their own. Then I wasn't sure if I felt sorrier for Daddy or the Leewoods for always having to ask for help. I knew Daddy and Mama didn't have much cash, but I also knew Daddy would give what little he had to help someone who was down on their luck. The Leewoods were certainly that!

Again we reported about our day or something else on our minds. Daddy asked about my herd with a bit of mischief in his voice. I told the family I saw Sam wave at me from where he was watching my herd at Smith Canyon. No one seemed to disbelieve me, so I continued reporting my herd was doing really well and getting fatter every day because the grass there was so tall and good. I felt validated when no one discredited my sighting of Sam. To me he was as real as anyone else in my seven-year-old world. I was glad Sam was so much like Daddy because that meant he was good in every way.

How excited I was the next day when Daddy told Wendy, Jim and me that we could go into Montpelier with him if we got our work done. Kari and Lucy had invited their entire 4-H club to our house for their meeting and demonstration. Mama was going to help the 4-H leader demonstrate for the group how to put a zipper in a skirt. Ugh! She didn't mind having the younger kids play in the yard at home where she could keep an eye on them.

It was a pleasant thing to be seven. I was big enough to go most places and do lots of things, yet I wasn't considered one of the little kids. My status was perfect. I was big when I wanted the benefits, but sort of small if there were really hard things to do. I could weave in and out of whichever deal suited me best. I didn't mean to be manipulative. I just wanted to be able to do the things I loved and avoid the things I didn't love. Was that so different from what most people, even adults, try to do?

Mama braided fresh braids for Wendy and me. Jim washed his face and put on a clean shirt. Mama didn't want us to look like hillbillies when we went to town and people saw us. We rode in the front of the truck with Daddy. He whistled part of the time as he drove along, happy but deep in thought.

Our first stop was at the UpTown tire shop, where Daddy let us out after we agreed to stay close to him. He opened the tailgate and pulled John Leewood's two flat tires to the edge of the truck bed. One at a time he lifted them out. He wheeled one in and Jim wheeled the other one into the open shop door. Jim liked being Daddy's wingman. Of course Wendy and I were just there as part of the committee, mostly to observe. There were two or three men working inside. A car was on a hoist up in the air a couple of feet with its tires off. I thought how strange it looked with just the little hubs. They seemed so small compared to the tires. It made me smile because I had never seen one with all the tires off at once. One of the working men looked at Wendy and me and winked. We were pleased but stood bashfully behind Daddy and Jim.

The shop smelled like a combination of rubber, grease and cement. I drank in the smell and liked it. One of the men came over to where we stood in the doorway. He was a tall, robust man in bib overalls with a ruddy, pleasant face. Daddy told him he had two tires that needed repair and asked if we could leave them. The man eyed the tires. He ran his rough, dirty fingers across the almost non-existent tread and asked if they were Daddy's. Daddy replied he brought them in for a neighbor. The man looked them over again, rubbing his stubby chin whiskers. He told Daddy they were hardly worth trying to patch, but he would try. He said to come back in an hour to pick them up.

We drove across town and across the railroad tracks to the feed store, where Daddy got a bag of lamb pellets for Monroe and some oyster shells and laying mash for the chickens. He also got some bags of rolled oats and a couple blocks of salt. Wendy, Jim and I watched a big grain elevator draw grain way up high, and some other interesting things. Our next stop was the grocery store to get a few things for

Mama and a box of supplies to take to Slim and Beatrice. The grocer always used a cardboard box for the groceries. Once in a while he also used a paper sack for lettuce and other soft things.

The store was always so fun to go in because it was alley after alley of cans and bottles and boxes of everything imaginable to eat. It was almost more than a child's mind could absorb. At the feed store as well as the grocery store, Daddy visited with several customers and the cashiers. They talked a lot about the bank robbers and their whereabouts. I liked to listen but was terribly distracted by the hugeness of everything around me while we were in town. I realized probably the best time for me to learn about what he knew was when Daddy gave his latest reports to Mama. Then I could listen and understand better.

We returned to the UpTown shop and got the Leewoods' tires. Daddy went in alone because he bought us ice cream cones and we needed to sit still to eat them. We hardly spoke a word as we licked the sweet, cold treat. He was gone for what seemed a long time. At least it was longer than it took us to eat our ice cream cones. Just as we voted on getting out and going in, Daddy came out wheeling one of the tires and the man in the bibbed overalls wheeling the other one. Down went the tailgate and in went the tires. As Daddy always did, he shook hands with the man and we headed for home. It was a nice trip to town but Daddy wasn't whistling as we drove along. He seemed deep in thought about something.

Jim and Daddy unloaded the things he bought at the feed store and carried them into the granary. Monroe heard the granary door open and bleated because he knew Jim might bring him some pellets. They had become buddies. Daddy carried the big box of groceries into the kitchen and Wendy and I carried the smaller box and the paper sack. Daddy sorted out what he would be taking to Slim and Beatrice. Mama put the other things away in her kitchen as she and Daddy talked.

I was about to go outside to play with the other kids when I heard them discussing the bank robbery. I sat quietly in the back of the kitchen where I could hear. Daddy summarized all he gathered from people he talked to in town. It seemed two of the robbers had been apprehended in the Wind River Mountains of Wyoming, but the third one was nowhere to be found and the money was also missing. The bank announced a reward of five thousand dollars to anyone who found and returned the money. The authorities supposed the third man must have gone into Montana or the Dakotas so officers were still searching. It was a relief to me to know the man was far away. Mama and Daddy seemed relieved too.

*Eve rides behind her brother on the far left. Two other siblings join Daddy and Charlie the mule on the right.*

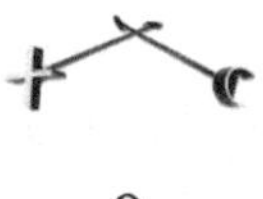

# 9

# A BEARY SCARY ENCOUNTER

I wondered how Sam was doing with my herd and if he might come around later that day. It seemed that he always showed up when I had news to give him. He was one of the constant factors in my life at that time. At supper I reported to Daddy I hadn't seen Sam all day but would see him soon. Daddy told the older kids they could go with him to Slim and Beatrice's camp the next morning. I could scarcely sleep because I was thinking about maybe being able to go. How I loved those adventures in the mountains!

It was no big surprise the next morning that the big sisters, Kari and Lucy, had other plans and didn't want to go to Slim and Beatrice's camp. Actually I was glad because that meant almost for sure I would be included in the ones chosen to go. Mama usually wanted the smaller kids closer to home where she could keep an eye on them.

Generally the yard and surrounding trees in the neighborhood held enough adventure for them. At least it did for Ginny, Mason and Nancy. The little boys, Mack and Little Larry, were happy and busy playing near Mama whether she was in the garden or kitchen. Daddy made Wendy, Jim and me his team for the day. We hurried to get our morning chores done. Daddy packed the supplies in the saddle bags and one other gunny sack he tied on Charlie behind the saddle. We didn't need the pack saddles this time because there was less to take.

As Daddy had done on other trips, he tied the horses behind the truck and they trotted along to Sage Canyon and the homestead cabin. That was our starting point for the trail ride. He took the two repaired tires and gave them to Mr. Leewood. As we got far enough north to see Smith Canyon in the distance, I thought again of Sam, my faithful herder, and hoped he was on a ridge somewhere watching us move along in the truck. If he saw us, even if we were smaller than a dot to him in the distance, he would know I was probably with Daddy and he would smile.

We headed up Sage Canyon Lane. When we got to the cabin Daddy pulled up and stopped. Sure enough, the Leewood's old beat-up truck was still sitting there, jacked up on one quarter waiting a tire. But it seemed rather quiet. No one came out to greet Daddy. He knocked on the door. Then he pounded on the door. He stepped off the porch and hollered into the mountain side, "Anybody home?" The reply was an echo and then a softer echo, then silence. Daddy lifted the tires out of his truck and put them both in the bed of the Leewood's truck, careful not to jar the jack loose.

We got our jackets and canteens—always standard, must-have gear on every ride. We tied them to the saddles and Daddy made assignments. He would ride Red Wing who was still a little jumpy. Wendy and I would double up on Pomp, and Jim would ride single on Charlie the mule because he was already carrying all the supplies. Daddy looked at the sun and told us we needed to get started before it got too hot. He always told time by the sun. So he led, then Wendy and I, with Jim bringing up the rear on old sure-footed Charlie.

We rode single file as we did before, listening to the breeze in the needles of the pines. I noticed how the wind makes a different sound in the pines than it does in quaking aspen or cottonwoods. The forest smells and sounds filled my senses as they always did. Occasionally a chipmunk or tree squirrel darted across in front of us. I wondered if there were bigger animals we couldn't see, but who could see us. I felt sure there were. Daddy had spoken of shooting a bear along that trail a few years earlier. The hide was back home in the shed. Most of all that morning I felt joy at being out in nature, riding along with Daddy leading us safely along the trail.

We visited some as we rode, but each of us was absorbing every sight and sound that surrounded us. At one point Jim hollered ahead to Daddy and asked if we were near the place where Sundance died. Daddy hollered back it was somewhere through there. He didn't ever really show us or tell us exactly where that happened or where Sundance was laid to rest. I think he thought it was best that we each dealt with it in our own imaginations and let it be.

It was always a little scary to me to go through the rough rocky area because the horses' feet sometimes slid a little on the rocks. Soon we passed that area and came to the opening where Slim and Beatrice's camp home was. This time as we approached the clearing, Beatrice came running toward us from the tent. She was talking a mile a minute, telling Daddy her Honey Slim was hurt and in the tent. Daddy dismounted and hurried to the tent. We got down and held the horses' reins as they nibbled the grass.

Daddy was in the tent for several minutes, so we tied the reins to the low brush near the trees and ventured to the tent. We could see Slim lying on their camp bed. He was in his red long johns with one leg elevated on a rolled-up blanket. Beatrice was fluttering over and around him like a moth by a flame, unable to land, unable to move away. Daddy told her sternly but kindly to sit down and tell him what happened. She sat. With tears she poured out the story.

Late yesterday as the sheep settled down for the night, bedded in the grass, Slim and Beatrice were slowly moving through the early shadows back toward camp when a black bear rose up in the trail on its hind legs and roared at them. Beatrice was able to stay on her terrified horse, but Slim's horse bucked him off and he landed on his leg, twisting it at a bad angle. His horse ran back to camp. Beatrice was able to help her Honey Slim get up on her horse and she led it back to camp. As they went one way, the frightened bear took off in the opposite direction. The night deepened as Slim's lower leg became swollen, discolored and more painful.

Telling the story seemed to calm Beatrice down somewhat. She must have spent a worrisome night thinking of the bear and knowing Slim was hurt. Daddy carefully felt the bones in Slim's leg and eventually made the diagnosis it was probably a bad sprain but no broken bones. Just hearing Daddy say that out loud also helped Beatrice relax.

As the morning light flooded into the opening of their big tent, it illuminated her face. It seemed that under the unruly, wild gray hair and the sun-seasoned skin and toothless mouth, there was a kind, likable and even vulnerable lady. Her kindness was all directed toward her Honey Slim but nonetheless it was there. I wondered if she had children of her own. Was she somebody's mother? It was in the moments of that morning I started to see her as a special human being, not just a peculiar, strange sidekick to our sheepherder. In my seven-year-old mind I dubbed her "Lady Beatrice." But that would be my secret.

Jim helped Daddy unload the supplies for Slim and Beatrice and carry them to the open tent. She was glad for the food, soap and other things we brought them. Then Daddy and Jim rode on ahead to check the salt troughs and water tank, since Slim was banged up. There was a tiny spring not far from the tent where Slim and Beatrice got their drinking water. While Daddy and Jim were gone during the next hour, Wendy and I pitched in and helped Beatrice bring a bucket of water to their tent and gathered firewood sticks which we put in a pile next to their camp.

I thought it seemed like a fun thing to live in a tent as they did, getting water from a spring and cooking over a fire each day. But then I thought of the dark nights, the bears and coyotes, and I was glad for my bed at home, snuggled next to my many sisters. I could almost hear Mama kneeling by my bed saying her prayer. I was glad our visit to camp was just that—a visit.

Beatrice had us peel potatoes while she fried some small pieces of lamb meat in her cast iron skillet on the fire. We sliced the potatoes into pieces and she put them in the other frying pan. They sizzled. We visited while waiting for Daddy and Jim to come back. She kept a cold cloth on Slim's swollen leg. He slept and seemed more at ease now that someone had come to their rescue.

While the food simmered we sat just inside the tent on blocks of wood and visited with Beatrice. The fresh mountain air flowed through the tent. She smiled her toothless smile as she told us about being a girl in a place called Sonora, far away in Mexico. Her family was poor and would have been happy to have such a nice tent to live in and enough food to eat each day. Living like that was hard for me to imagine. I had never gone hungry one day in my whole life even though I knew Mama and Daddy didn't have much money. I couldn't imagine being so poor there were days with no food at all.

Beatrice smiled warmly as she told us about those things. It seemed the brown checks of her faded blouse made her hazel eyes brighter. There was a lightness about Beatrice. It was an invisible kind of kindness, not necessarily seen, but felt until you could *almost* see it. It was hard to describe, but I felt happy for privately dubbing her Lady Beatrice. Now that she was more relaxed about Slim, the lines in her face seemed softer too.

The food was beginning to smell delicious. Soon we heard the horses coming back down the trail to the camp. We all sat in the shade of the trees and enjoyed Beatrice's hospitality for lunch. Among the items we brought to her were freshly picked carrots and a loaf of Mama's bread. Daddy told her not to use the bread on us, but to save it for her and Slim.

Beatrice offered us a new food with a strong scent sizzling in the skillet—small round meatballs. She forked a bunch onto Daddy's plate and then, winking at him, offered some to us. Daddy called them "lamb fries" and said we probably wouldn't like them. I had eaten French fries, of course, but not lamb fries, and wondered what part of a sheep they came from.

Slim was sitting up and seemed able to hobble around with help. That was a huge relief to Daddy. He worried he would have to send someone else up to help with the herd until Slim's leg healed. But it seemed it would be okay with Beatrice's help. We thanked her for her kindness and the meal. Daddy went into the tent and visited with Slim. When we left, Beatrice stood at the edge of the clearing and waved to us as we started down the trail. I thought how brave she was to be left there with an injured husband, a herd of sheep to tend, and obviously predators around her. I knew Lady Beatrice would be okay.

It seemed like every time we were near the trees I remembered that day I saw the stranger in the blue shirt in the pines above us and how I later found a blue button in the cabin. Somehow I knew they were connected, but didn't know how to sort it out. At first I wondered if the man was one of the robbers from Wyoming because I was really frightened when we heard about it. But then news came through the valley that two of them were caught in Wyoming and the third one probably had gone into the Dakotas. I still had the blue button at home in a safe place in my drawer where I could get it out and hold it and think about it. I guess buttons get lost in all kinds of strange places.

When we got down the canyon to the cabin, smoke was coming from the chimney. The old Leewood truck had its tire back on and was parked at a different angle. I knew Daddy would want to talk to Mr. Leewood. We wearily dismounted and tied our horses to the back of Daddy's truck. The water from our canteens was refreshing. Jim stretched his legs by jaunting through the chokecherry bushes and up the hillside just because boys like to run and climb. Wendy and I were glad to drop in the shade of a tall sagebrush near the cabin and listen to the men talking.

Mr. Leewood gave Daddy some coins to pay for the tire repair. I doubt it came anywhere near the real cost. I also knew Daddy was reluctant to take anything, believing that was probably all the money Mr. Leewood had to his name. But I think Daddy wanted Mr. Leewood to feel good about trying to pay his way.

Mr. Leewood and his wife Dora had been looking for wild strawberries earlier in the morning when we stopped by and left our truck. They had walked along the lower hillside all the way to Skunk Hollow and found a nice mess of berries. They had also gone to Montpelier for a few groceries after he changed the tire. Whatever Dora was cooking smelled good. I thought of Mama cooking supper and felt ready to head for home. I wondered about Sam and my herd. It was time for him to stop in and visit. Perhaps he would come after supper tonight when I was alone at home.

Sure enough, later that evening after supper was over and I was sitting on the back porch, Sam came and talked to me. He was on his way home to his wife. I told him all the happenings of the last few days. He listened and nodded from time to time. He asked if I was having a good summer. I told him I was still concerned about that man in the blue shirt I had seen a month earlier in Sage Canyon. He said not to worry, it was probably just one of the trappers.

I asked if he had seen anyone around Smith Canyon near my herd. Sam said he hadn't seen anyone unusual and that my lambs were really getting big. He had never seen such a good herd. I told him about Daddy's sheepherder, Slim, getting injured and all about the bear. Sam listened but didn't seem alarmed. He was too brave to ever be frightened of anything. Then he left as quietly as he had come. I knew he had to get home to his pretty wife with the big hat. It always made me feel calmer and happier when I talked to Sam. As always the trail ride had made us really tired. After a warm, soapy bath we all slept well. All worries over bank robbers and bears were forgotten.

# 10

# LOST

The next morning we helped Mama weed the big garden before the sun got too hot. She watered it the day before while we were gone, so the soil was damp and perfect for pulling up long-rooted weeds. We asked if we could take a wheelbarrow of weeds to the chickens. She usually didn't like them to eat green feed because it was seen and tasted in their eggs, but this time she said it was okay.

Ginny, Mason and Nancy filled their arms with weeds and loaded them into the wheelbarrow until it was heaping. Jim and Wendy pushed the huge load out to the barnyard with the rest of us bouncing along behind them. I opened the chicken wire gate into the run and pushed the wheelbarrow inside. The chickens were a bit frightened by all the commotion at first, but once we started pulling off the weeds and throwing them out, they came running and clucking. They were like kids at an Easter egg hunt, running and pecking and running and pecking at the wonderful delicacies strewn before them.

We weeded until we were hot and tired. As we left the side yard and looked back at the garden with its dark, damp soil and straight green rows, it looked quite beautiful. Mama picked an armful of carrots and fresh beets and washed the dirt off in the hose by the back door. I knew they would be on the supper table before the day was finished.

Monroe heard all the activity and called to Jim, who put the little lamb halter on him and proudly led him around the yard for us to see. I was amazed at how Monroe was growing. It must have been because of the lamb pellets Jim was always feeding him and the green feed from the side pasture. The other lambs weren't as friendly since they had gone off the bottle and straight onto feed. But Monroe was a different story. He and Jim were best pals.

A day or two later Daddy asked if we wanted to ride with him out to the cabin and to check the fields. Kari and Lucy wanted to stay home in the cool house, but Mama said no. She wanted all of us to pick wild strawberries. We found some buckets and other containers we put in the back of the truck. We all loaded in with Mama, Daddy, Mack and Little Larry in the front. The rest of us rode in the back, even Kari and Lucy who had tied bandannas around their hair. I wasn't sure I wanted to ever be a teenager because it seemed like it took lots of extra work and care. I liked being seven years old and free as the wind.

Since we had no horses tied behind the truck, we moved along at a decent pace with the breeze blowing in our faces and the summer sun warming us. The metal buckets and gallon cans in the box clanked and jangled with the vibration of the truck.

Mama had never met the Leewoods. I was curious to see what she thought of them. We pulled up to the cabin and parked next to their beat-up old truck. Mr. Leewood stepped out on the porch. Most of the kids ran up the hillside at our favorite running place. I stayed in the back with Kari and Lucy so I could hear what the adults said. Then Dora Leewood joined her husband on the porch in a faded shirt-waist dress and a worn and tired apron around her waist.

Mama climbed out of the truck cab and walked around to Daddy's side. Mr. Leewood introduced his wife to Mama. Both women smiled politely at one another. Daddy asked how their plans were coming along. Mr. Leewood explained that he did a few days' work for a rancher west of town so he could earn some traveling money. He asked Daddy if it was okay for them to stay until he could stabilize a little better financially. Daddy agreed a little longer would be okay since they seemed to be taking care of the place. Daddy would never turn someone away who needed help. And what did it really hurt anyway for them to be there? The cabin had been empty for a long time.

Daddy told the Leewoods we came to pick wild strawberries, to which they both exclaimed the foothills were covered with them as far north as they walked the other day. Daddy whistled and the kids all came racing down the hill to the truck. We got our containers, Mama paired us off in twos and threes and told us where to start looking. She kept Mack and Little Larry with her.

We were to go no farther north than Skunk Hollow and to stay low on the hill. Daddy told us when we heard the truck horn honk it meant to come back. Away we scattered, chattering about who would get the most and where the biggest berries always were. As excited as I was to find a plump, sweet strawberry to eat, I was more nervous about accidentally getting a wood tick. That always haunted me. But each and every time we went to the mountains we got a thorough checking over by Mama when we got home.

It seemed like Wendy, Jim and I were always together, partly because of our status as the "middle kids," but mostly because our interests were so similar and our experiences so intertwined. On strawberry-picking day it was no surprise we three were together with our metal buckets combing the lower hillside for berries. Berries were plentiful, growing underfoot all along the way. We didn't talk much except to express delight about the berries. We picked and gleaned, picked and gleaned. A time or two my little bucket tipped and I had to gather my berries up and brush them off. I thought that was like having to pick them twice so I became more careful as I learned how to juggle the bucket and my picking.

I was telling Wendy my little bucket was getting full, but she didn't answer back. I repeated myself. Total silence. We had all been crawling down low to the ground, so I stood to see if I could see her and Jim. The bushes around me were over my head. I moved a few feet in every direction trying to see out. I called and called but to no avail. If I went up the hill a ways I could look down and get my bearings and see Jim and Wendy. But which way was up? The ground where I stood seemed level. I pushed my way through more bushes but everything was flat. I couldn't see out. I turned around so many times I lost my bearings about which way led back to the cabin.

Fear gripped me. I had never been mixed up or lost before in the canyon. I thought I knew it like the back of my hand because we were there so often. But we had wandered quite a way north when we started picking berries. Now I didn't know where anybody was and the more I tried to get out of the tall bushes, the more confused I became. I was sure I would hear the truck horn honk before long and that would help me get my bearings. In the meantime I decided to walk towards the direction of the cabin. I picked my way through the dense underbrush which scratched my neck and arms as I pushed through. I couldn't find a trail of any kind. It was a total thicket and way over my head.

As much as I considered myself a brave, capable girl, I felt a rush of panic race through me and I started to cry. But I kept pushing and pushing through the bushes. I was sure I would eventually come to an opening and be able to run to the cabin, the truck, and the safety of Mama's arms. She would gather me up and kiss my tears away and hold me tight until the fear drained out of me.

The bushes got thicker. Little did I know I had wandered way beyond Skunk Hollow and farther north into a narrow draw that led me more eastward. Its grade was so gradual I assumed I was still on level ground fairly near the cabin, but actually I had wandered a great distance in the opposite direction! I listened for the horn. I listened for the sound of my brothers and sisters. All I heard was forest silence. The bushes were so thick I couldn't see pine trees or even the sky anymore. I couldn't hear the sound of the breeze in the pine needles. I sat down in the dirt and bushes and cried loud and hard until there were no more tears. Exhausted, I collapsed into sleep, a respite for my agony.

The cold and shivering of my shoulders awakened me. It was pitch dark. I had no idea how long I slept, but the daylight was gone. The remembrance of picking berries and getting lost swirled around in my mind like a bad dream. Then reality sank in. I really was lost and it was night. Then my shivering was a mixture of being cold and thinking of bears.

Suddenly Sam was there, smiling and telling me I would be okay and to not worry. He would watch over me and watch for bears and scare them away if they came near. He also told me he would ride back and tell Mama and Daddy I was okay so they wouldn't worry. I knew how Mama worried over us. Then Sam was gone as silently as he had appeared. That's the way he was, but I felt much better after he talked to me.

I stayed huddled under the bushes for what seemed like an eternity. How did everything get so wet during the night? I remembered how dew got on our grassy lawn at home early in the morning and figured this wetness must be forest dew.

It made me even colder. I didn't have my jacket with me because we were picking in the warmth of the day and there was no need for it then. Thinking of the jacket made me recall how Daddy always told us when we were on a trail ride to bring a jacket and a canteen of water. Then I started thinking how good a drink of water would be. I put my tongue on my lips and felt dryness.

The darkness slowly began to lessen. Was it morning? It must be. I started pushing through the brush again, sure I was headed toward the cabin and familiar territory. The light that seeped through the bushes was still dim. It must have been barely light. I walked where I could and crawled where I couldn't stand upright. At some point I lost my bucket of berries but didn't want to turn back. No, I was determined to get back to the cabin if I had to crawl all the way. That's what I had to do in some places.

The bushes thinned enough that I could see rays of the morning sun filtering through their leaves. Oh, joy! How I appreciated the daylight. I moved toward the brightness of the sun, not realizing I was headed east instead of south back to the cabin. I went at a snail's pace, but nonetheless was moving. After what seemed like a long and tiring time, I stopped and sat down to rest. I could hear the trickle of water. I moved slowly to the right a little bit and saw a tiny clearing where a little stream bubbled out of the mossy rocks.

A mother deer and her fawn were drinking. When they heard my movement their heads jerked up and off they bounded out of sight. I crawled out of the bushes and went to the water. Gratefully I knelt on the wet grass and sucked water into my dry mouth. We had been told not to drink from mountain water unless Daddy approved it, but I felt he would be okay with this. It quenched my thirst but made my empty stomach growl for something more.

I stood up in the clearing and stretched my arms. It felt good to be in the full light of the sun and soak in its early warmth. From the spring a little trail led forward. I was glad to walk that way. It was narrow, undoubtedly an animal trail to the water hole. But walking toward the sun was more appealing than crawling back through the underbrush I had just come through. I walked along with a bit of new confidence, feeling I would for sure now be found. I could see the tall pines on either side of the draw. I felt confused because that was not the way it looked going down from Skunk Hollow back to the cabin. The light and the trail led me forward. I was determined to find my way out. I never, ever wanted to spend another lonely, frightening night in the canyon bushes.

*Evie in pigtails with three siblings.*

## 11

## THE PROMISE

The trail widened somewhat and the bushes were farther back off the trail. I went around a little bend and there in front of me right in the trail was a huge mountain of a man. He had a thick black beard and seemed as surprised as I was. I tried to scream, but only air escaped my lips.

He could see I was trembling and backed up a step or two to assure me he meant no harm. He put his hands out and up as he backed away. He spoke first, asking if I was lost. I choked out that I was. He said not to worry because he knew how to get out of the woods. I studied him skeptically. The sun was against his back and in my eyes. To my horror I realized he was the man in the blue plaid shirt I had seen earlier that summer near the cabin. The same one we had run into on one of our trail rides. My heart leapt into my throat and began pounding.

Then I saw what truly terrified me. The third button-hole down in his blue plaid shirt was missing the button! What would he have said or done if I had told him his missing button was at home in my drawer? Why had he been in Daddy's cabin?

He got down on his knees and said to not be afraid. When I could see him more clearly he didn't really look frightening at all. He said he was looking for something he lost a while back. He said he would tell me how to reach safety if I promised not to tell anyone he was there. It sounded like a good deal to me. My only thought was to be found. He made me say "I promise." I croaked it out.

If I stayed right on the trail and kept going toward the sun, he said, I would come to a sheepherder's camp and they would help me. I didn't know there were any other sheep herds in the canyon except Daddy's. For an instant I was confused. Then I realized he must mean Slim and Beatrice's camp! I couldn't believe I was anywhere near their camp. Had I gone that far north and east? He bade me farewell and went into the brush where I couldn't see him anymore. I started walking, this time with real hope in my soul.

I walked for what seemed a long while. Soon I could hear the low lulling of sheep and an occasional tinkle of a sheep bell. Sure enough I was getting near someone's herd. Then I heard the distant sound of voices chattering to each other—in Spanish! A few steps more and the trail opened wide into a familiar clearing. There were Slim and Beatrice sitting on their stumps by the tent, eating breakfast. I had come into their camp from the back side.

They both jumped up when they saw me. I must have been a fright to look at but they immediately recognized me. Beatrice ran to me, picked me up and held me. I began crying uncontrollably. I sobbed into her forest-green top while she stroked my back, saying "poor baby, poor baby" a thousand times. She rocked me back and forth and I cried until I was limp. Finally my sobs subsided enough to speak. She asked why I was there. I told her about the strawberries and how I got lost and it was dark and I was scared and—but I paused and *did not* tell her about the man on the trail. *A promise is a promise.*

She repeated each of my sentences in Spanish to which Slim shook his head up and down and nodded with understanding. Beatrice set me down on a stump and spooned oatmeal into a metal dish for me. She poured a touch of sweet canned milk on it and handed it to me. I ate like I had never seen food. I could feel the warmth of it going down my throat and calming my hungry stomach. She gave me water to drink.

She and Slim talked to each other in Spanish while I ate. I noticed Slim limped only slightly on the leg he injured several days earlier. At least he was up and walking on it without help. He went to their horses who were hobbled and eating nearby. He took the hobbles off one of them and put a bridle on it and led it over near the side of the tent where their gear was stacked. He put a saddle blanket and saddle on it as Beatrice buzzed around cleaning up the meal and dishes. She told me to sit in the sun and rest. I really did feel tired when I thought about it.

They conversed in Spanish in what seemed to be an agreeable sort of way. Beatrice offered to take me down to my parents. She knew they would be terribly worried. Suddenly it occurred to me what a terrible night of fear Mama and Daddy and the family must have experienced, wondering where I had gone.

Beatrice put her foot in the stirrup and mounted. Then Slim lifted me up with ease and placed me behind the saddle. Instinctively I held tightly to Beatrice's waist. How grateful I was for Lady Beatrice. She tightened the strings on her straw hat and urged the horse forward. Somehow I didn't see her any more as a toothless, graying, wrinkled woman. At that moment she was my gallant heroine who would return me to my mother's arms.

She chatted and chattered all the way down the canyon, talking about my family, her Honey Slim, the sheep, and her time as a little girl in Mexico. I know now it was her way to keep me distracted and calm. The time passed and finally we heard the sound of people. We soon saw smoke from the old cabin chimney. My heart leapt with joy! Someone from high on the mountain yelled down to the others that we were coming. There were yelps and yahoos all through the trees as a dozen or more men descended from the hillsides to the cabin.

As we approached I saw Mama standing by our truck. She wiped her hands across her eyes and ran to meet us. In a matter of seconds I was in her arms just as I had imagined. She truly was holding me and loving me. I felt her warm tears fall on my neck. And the fear, the terrible fear of last night, at last drained from me.

Beatrice stood, holding her horse and talking to the others, telling how I wandered into their camp this morning and how they fed me and brought me down to the cabin. Mama sat on the truck seat and I stayed on her lap a long, long time. Several other trucks were parked in the bottom of the canyon. Mama and Daddy waited for everyone to gather back at the cabin. Daddy shook hands with each man who helped search. He thanked them over and over, as I did in my heart.

*When they saw smoke from the old cabin chimney Evie's "heart leapt with joy!"*

*Evie with little sister.*

## 12

## SAFELY HOME

All the people left in their trucks and headed off down the dusty road. Daddy and Mama thanked Beatrice at least a hundred times. She assured them Slim's leg was healing and the herd was doing fine. Mama got out of the truck and gave Beatrice a big hug. Then Beatrice got on her horse, grinned her warm toothless smile, and headed back up the canyon, turning to wave at us before she went out of sight around the bend.

Daddy and Mama told the Leewoods good-bye and we headed for home. I was surprised none of the other kids were with them. Mama said they had chores at home. Later I realized my siblings were left there because the searchers didn't know what the outcome would be. Daddy and Mama were protecting them from what might have been a very different ending to the story. It made me think of bears and the man on the trail who helped me find my way out. I knew I could never tell anyone about that. I was glad Sam had stopped by to offer hope on the worst of all the nights of my life.

When we arrived home all the family came running to greet us as we got out of the truck. The big girls cried and everyone cheered. I was somewhat of a celebrity for the rest of the day. Mama ran a big tubful of warm water. She unbraided my hair and washed me from the top of my head to the tip of my toes. No one could have been more relieved than I when she announced there were no ticks. I felt so clean and thankful and happy. It was like all the feelings of good that I ever felt in my life were rolled up inside me and warming me all over.

Throughout the day the phone rang and I heard Mama tell people I was safely home and thanked them for calling. I stayed close to Mama. It wasn't that I was really afraid now. It was just that being close to her made me feel more secure and safe. After two or three days Mama asked what I was thinking about since I was being extra quiet. I told her I was thinking about the lambs and the swing and things like that, yet I didn't want to go outside to see the lambs or actually play on the swing. I kept thinking about what could have happened on that trail and about the man I promised. And I didn't want to talk about it.

On about the fourth day Mama said she was taking me to the doctor. Now that isn't something a kid wants to hear. I wasn't sick. What was she thinking? She braided my hair and had me wear my nice school dress and anklets and my Sunday shoes. Daddy drove us and again I sat on Mama's lap most of the way to Montpelier. The three of us walked into the clinic and sat down in the waiting room. The nurse in white came out and motioned it was our turn to go in. Daddy stayed in a chair, reading a magazine and visiting with other patients.

The nurse took Mama and me into a little room that had two big chairs and a little table with a little chair by it. On the table was a stack of blank paper and a container with lots of color crayons. Soon a pretty lady dressed in light green came in and talked to Mama. This wasn't the doctor. I knew Dr. Reed, he was a man and this was not Dr. Reed. The lady in green smiled at me and said she was Dr. Callie. She held out her hand, and after she shook Mama's hand, she turned to shake mine. But I pulled back. I had never been shy but on that day I didn't really want anyone else talking to me or shaking my hand at all. She still smiled.

Dr. Callie sat in the other big chair. I was still on Mama's lap. They talked about families and the weather and all sorts of things. Mentally I shut them out until Dr. Callie asked if I would like to draw a picture for her. I was reluctant even though drawing with crayons was truly one of my favorite things to do on our quiet evenings at home. In a gentle way Dr. Callie suggested I draw a picture of what I had been doing the last few days. I slid down and sat on the little chair. Looking at Mama for reassurance, I placed a paper on the table in front of me. As they continued to visit, I felt like the focus was off me and I relaxed enough to concentrate on my picture.

First I drew a bright red strawberry with a green leaf. I drew the cabin with smoke coming out of the chimney. I drew lots of smoke. I wanted someone to be home in the cabin. I drew a mother deer and her fawn standing in some blue water. I drew a horse with a gray-haired lady sitting on it. She wore a yellow hat. Down in the corner I drew a very tall man. I colored the buttons blue, very blue. Then I put a moon at the top of the page. I gave the paper to Mama and crawled back up on her lap.

Dr. Callie and Mama looked at the drawing together. Silence. Then Dr. Callie told me what a nice picture it was and she thanked me for it. She asked if she could keep it and I agreed. I really didn't want to be reminded about that night anyway. The nurse in white took me back out to wait with Daddy while Mama stayed in the room and talked with Dr. Callie. Soon Mama came out and we left the clinic.

We went to the grocery store. Mama asked what I wanted to eat for supper. It wasn't even my birthday and I got to choose what to have for supper! I said fried chicken, so Mama got some in the meat department. Usually we had our own home-grown chickens, but Daddy hadn't butchered any lately. Our trip home was quiet. I knew Mama was probably full of information to give Daddy, but she hesitated to say anything in front of me. Seven-year-olds aren't entirely clueless.

I changed into my play clothes and for the first time in several days I climbed into the tire swing and let Wendy push me higher and higher. It felt good to be floating above my world if only for a few seconds at a time. Once I even heard myself laugh out loud. I felt free. I felt like I had come back from a long, scary journey. And I had.

Daddy gave the blessing on the food that night and also said we were thankful we were all home together again around the table. It held new meaning for all of us since the day I got lost. Mama offered her prayer at my bedside every night for a whole week.

For several days I stayed closer to home. Even when Daddy said we could go with him to the fields, I chose to stay near Mama. I helped her in the garden and the kitchen. I even fed Monroe his lamb pellets. But I never dared to put Monroe's halter on him and lead him into the yard the way Jim did. I was pretty strong for my age, but not strong enough to hold onto the likes of Monroe when his mind was set on going somewhere.

Summer reached its absolute peak. The flowers in Mama's flowerbed were taking on rich, vibrant colors. There were vegetables galore from the garden. It seemed like I was always snapping string beans or shelling peas for supper. There were beets and beet greens, carrots and more carrots. Once in a while Mama had me take a wheelbarrow of carrot tops or pea shells and put them over the fence into the horse pasture. I petted the horses' nose and recalled our many trail rides. I thought maybe I would go with Daddy and the others the next time he offered. The horror of my night alone in the mountains was still very real, but the joy of the trail rides was starting to filter back through my mind. The big girls were busy giggling with their teenage friends or working on 4-H projects. The younger kids played in the yard.

Jim and Wendy built a great treehouse in the cottonwoods across the lane. It wasn't high enough to be scary, but high enough to feel like we were on a grand adventure when we played in it. We even lifted Little Larry into it a few times so he could have fun. Mama didn't like us doing that. He was too little to hold onto the ladder steps nailed to the trunk of the tree and he might fall. That's why we lifted him. But we minded Mama and mostly played in the treehouse when Little Larry was napping or busy somewhere in Mama's care.

Then one morning at breakfast Daddy asked each of us what was our most important thing to do that day. He was going to make a ride back up to Slim and Beatrice's camp and anyone big enough to ride a horse could go. Of course the big girls had no interest. Jim and Wendy volunteered in unison and looked at me. I wanted to go, but just couldn't quite get the words out for sure. I felt tongue-tied. Then with a bit of encouragement from Jim and Wendy and a kind look from Daddy, I joined the ranks. The younger kids chose to play at home. That was the way things usually divided up. Jim, Wendy and I were Daddy's middle trio who loved the adventures with him.

We hurried to do our chores. Pomp, Red Wing and Charlie were saddled and tied behind the truck. They were used to the routine and came along without a fuss. Daddy put a huge saddle-bag pack in the truck with supplies for Slim and Beatrice. We each kissed Mama good-bye and got in the truck. As usual, all three of us rode in the back. That was half the fun of summer and being in the country. I think sometimes Daddy half wished he were a kid and could sit back there with us.

As we rode along I could see Daddy looking to the right and left, scrutinizing each field and its growth. That's what farmers did. I looked north as we approached the canyons. I wondered when I would see Sam again. I wondered if my herd lambs were growing as fast as Monroe was growing. I knew they must be and knew Sam would be watching over them carefully.

Seeing the cabin, the hillsides, and the mountains again shocked me. A cold panic rose up inside and I felt stifled to breathe for a few moments. It was the memory of my terrible night flooding back into my mind. I started to cry softly. When we stopped at the cabin, Jim and Wendy told Daddy I was crying. He hurried and lifted me out and held me for a few minutes. The panic subsided and I was okay again. Daddy said it was just my mind remembering things and it would get easier each time I came to the cabin. I trusted him and pushed back the fear.

The Leewoods' truck was gone, but Daddy knocked on the door anyway. Mrs. Leewood opened the door in her timid way. Her husband was driving tractor for a few days for a farmer west of town. Daddy asked if things were going okay and she assured him they were fine.

Daddy put the pack-saddle on the back of Charlie behind Jim. Wendy and I rode double on Pomp as usual. As soon as Daddy made sure we had our jackets and water, he mounted Red Wing. He only shied a little bit which was progress. I can't imagine what Red Wing would have done if Daddy had put the big pack on him. He probably would have given us a real rodeo.

We clip-clopped our way up the familiar forest trail. The sights and sounds were always pleasant. It seemed the more trips we made the more the horses moved along in ideal trail-ride fashion with little coaxing.

*Daddy at his sheep camp.*

# 13

# MR. SCHUPE'S SECRET

When we came into the clearing at Slim and Beatrice's camp we could see they were talking to a man. I immediately recognized him as the tall man I met on the trail when I was lost. A mixture of fright and curiosity ran through me and I felt a shiver go up my back.

The conversation seemed pleasant and calm. We got off the horses and tied them up. Daddy walked over to where Slim, Beatrice and the tall man were standing on the other side of the clearing. I wanted desperately to hear what they were talking about. I felt I had a vested interest in the conversation because, after all, I was the first one to talk to him. But I knew my place was with Jim, Wendy and the horses. Of course I had kept my promise and never told anyone, not even Mama and Daddy, about seeing that man on the day I was lost. I still had the blue button. That had to be a clue to something.

When Beatrice saw Daddy walking toward them, she came to where we were standing by our horses. Her smile was warm and friendly. She reached down and patted my head and asked if I got rested up. I nodded and smiled up at her. It was like we had bonded in a way no one else would understand. She was the one who pulled me from my nightmare and took me back to Mama. She was forever my heroine, Lady Beatrice.

At her invitation we went over to the fire pit near the tent door and sat on the log and stumps they used for chairs.

She went back to where the men were standing and talking. I could tell Daddy was engrossed in what the man was saying. Slim, of course, waited for Beatrice to interpret most of it. When they were finished talking, the tall man left on the trail in back of the clearing where I came stumbling in on that dreadful morning. He disappeared into the darkness of the bushes and forest foliage. Daddy led Charlie closer to the tent before he lifted down the heavy pack. It was good to see Slim wasn't limping much. Slim and Beatrice unloaded the pack bag with delight. It was their new supply of cereal, flour, bacon, eggs, sugar and all kinds of items for their camp for the next while. I noticed two big Hershey chocolate bars like Daddy sometimes bought for us kids. Beatrice smiled wide at the sight of them.

Our visit was pleasant but not long. Daddy, Slim and Beatrice talked about how the sheep were doing. They saw the government trapper and he reported killing a few coyotes. The trapper had also seen a bear, probably the same one that caused Slim's accident. The trapper had the right to shoot a bear if it was bothering the sheep, which bears did sometimes. Usually they lived on berries and other meatless things, but occasionally a bear would kill sheep so they had to be watched closely.

When we got ready to leave they bade us a grateful farewell. Beatrice put her arm around my shoulder as we walked back to the horses. We would always be friends. We left and headed westward down the trail in our usual fashion with Daddy leading the way. I couldn't wait to get home so I could hear what Daddy would tell Mama about the tall man.

At the cabin we tied our horses to the back of the truck as always. Mrs. Leewood stood on her porch and waved as we loaded up and left on the dusty road. Daddy didn't stop to talk to her. Mr. Leewood was apparently still gone on his farming job because his truck was gone.

We three kids rode in the back and enjoyed the greenery of summer and the breeze that stirred the hot air as we moved along homeward to the south. I thought about Sam when I saw the mountains to the north. I was so glad to have a good sheep herder whom I could count on to watch my herd and report to me. My herd wasn't as big as Daddy's but it was important to me. I knew I could always trust Sam to be there when I needed him.

After taking the saddles off the horses, we all stood in front of the barn and laughed as Charlie rolled in the soft dirt: One, two, and three complete rollovers. Daddy declared he was worth three hundred dollars. Then Charlie stood and shook the dirt from his hide with an enormous shuddering that startled the chickens in the chicken run. They scurried in the opposite direction, squawking with feathers flying. We really laughed at that. The horses and Charlie were put into the pasture and we were ready to go inside the cool house out of the summer heat.

We arrived home awhile before supper, so we washed up and Mama checked us for ticks. Wendy and I got the creeps when Mama found one on the back of Jim's shirt. Mama didn't just take him outside and brush off the tick. She strategically removed it from the shirt with a little stick, then took it out by the back porch, lit a wooden match and cremated it. Sheep or wood ticks burrow their heads down into the skin and are hard to remove. They carry bad diseases such as Rocky Mountain Spotted Fever which makes people really sick.

Of course the little ones all came to watch the burning of the tick. Jim was a bit of a hero in their eyes for the moment. He spit on the ground and said it didn't scare him at all. He was greatly admired by all the little ones, including me. I was never happier than when I was with Jim and Wendy. They were the main orbit of my life.

After Daddy washed up and was sitting in the kitchen, he and Mama had quite a conversation about the tall man. The big girls were in another part of the house. Jim, Wendy and the others were playing in the trees. I was sitting on the shady back porch in the big wicker chair. Through the wooden screen door their voices wafted out and I heard every word.

Daddy settled in to tell Mama the whole story. The man's name was Norman Schupe. He was from Wyoming and knew all about the bank robbery. About a week after the heist, Mr. Schupe had been fishing in an isolated place along the river when he came across three men arguing. He hid in the willows and listened as their anger escalated into a knock-down, drag-out fight. While they were fighting and punching each other some distance away, he saw their belongings near him in the willows where they camped.

Among other things he spied a canvas bag about the size of a water bag. He peeked in and saw several packets of money in paper bills. He knew instantly that the men must have been the fugitive bank robbers. Mr. Schupe also knew a huge reward of five thousand dollars was offered to anyone who recovered the stolen money. He grabbed the money bag and his fishing gear and slinked off through the willows to hide.

He wanted to turn the money in to the authorities and get the reward to use for something very important. His young son had a crippled leg that could be improved with an operation that cost thousands of dollars. Mr. Schupe had no insurance and no way to pay for the operation until—maybe—now!

When the fight was over, he heard a commotion as the bandits discovered the money was gone and probably feared being caught. They grabbed their belongings, jumped into a car, and sped off. Mr. Schupe cautiously peeked through the willows at their campsite, now deserted. There was only mashed-down river grass where they had been, and no sign of a fire whose smoke could have given their location away.

He walked over to where they had been fighting. To his absolute horror, there was a man lying dead with a knife in his back. Mr. Schupe grabbed the money bag and his fishing gear and ran back to his own truck down the river, fearing they might come back looking for the bag. He drove aimlessly northward, passing through several small towns, planning to hide the money until he could be sure someone would believe where it came from. Otherwise authorities might assume he was part of the robbery gang.

He also drove along the dusty road at the base of the mountains until he found a place to hide it. He didn't tell Daddy or Slim and Beatrice where it was. He wanted to talk to the sheriff and convince him to believe his story before turning over the money. A big problem was that after two bank robbers were caught, Mr. Schupe thought he might be accused of being the third robber, and he had no way of proving differently. He asked Daddy to go with him to the sheriff and be a witness for him. Mama gasped at the thought! She didn't want Daddy to be involved in any way with such a mess.

I couldn't believe my young ears as I heard Daddy unfold the story to Mama. She did not want the kids to be told anything at all about this for now. Daddy agreed wholeheartedly. At that point I ran to the cottonwoods across the lane to be with my brothers and sisters, away from such terrible tales. I didn't want Mama and Daddy to know I was listening.

*Evie on far right with siblings.*

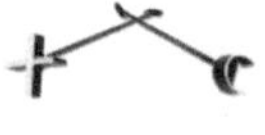

# 14

## CHARACTER WITNESS

At supper that night Daddy was unusually quiet. Mama tried to help fill the conversation gaps. I doubt if anyone else besides Mama and I even noticed. It was my turn to help wash the dishes and I did so, all the while deep in thought about what was going to happen next. More than once Wendy handed a dish back to me because I hadn't cleaned it well enough.

That evening we were all in the living room as usual. Mama sat mending. Daddy sat by the lamp with a newspaper in his hands. The rest of us busied ourselves with various play or quiet activities. I drew a picture of images twirling through my mind. I included a treehouse, not putting lots of bushes near it. I didn't want anyone hiding in the bushes even in my seven-year-old imagination.

I wanted to go out on the back porch in case Sam came by to talk. But that night I was even nervous to be out there alone. Why should I be afraid? The third robber was dead somewhere by the river and the other two had been nabbed. That is if Mr. Schupe's story was true. I guess I was a little like Red Wing: I jumped and spooked at things I didn't understand or see coming. Maybe with more time I would be less anxious. I already felt progress—until we heard Mr. Schupe's disconcerting tale. I really wanted to talk to Sam, who would make me feel better. But he didn't come that night.

After breakfast the next morning someone knocked on the back door. That wasn't unusual because people in the neighborhood used back doors generally. Mama wiped her hands on her apron and went through the back of the kitchen to the screen door. I heard a man's voice but didn't hear what he said. Mama told him Daddy had gone to irrigate a field and would be back about noon. I recognized the voice, it was Mr. Schupe.

When Mama came back in the kitchen I could tell she was a bit rattled, but I don't think any of the other kids noticed. I guess I knew too much for my own good. After hearing Mr. Schupe's tale, a lot that had happened took on a double meaning in my eyes. I almost felt like there was something hiding behind every bush and hidden in every conversation. I listened with deliberation to all of Mama and Daddy's conversations, trying to pick up some clue about what was going on.

Daddy came back from irrigating and changed from his muddy work clothes into his go-to-town clothes. He and Mama talked quietly in their bedroom, a place we generally weren't invited into. The door was usually open, but it was *their* place and we were taught to respect that. Without hearing what they said, I put two and two together in my mind. I supposed Mr. Schupe had come so he and Daddy could go to the sheriff together.

I wasn't far off. About half an hour later Mr. Schupe came to the back door again. Daddy put on his newer straw hat and went out. Together they walked to Daddy's truck. I rushed to the back porch to watch them drive away out of the barnyard and down the road. I could see Mr. Schupe's blue-gray truck parked by the outer gate to the barnyard. I thought it looked about as old and beat up as the Leewoods' old pick-up.

Mama was rather unsettled for the next couple of hours as she worked around the house and in the garden. She got after Jim for waiting until the sun was so hot before he started mowing the lawn. The mower was old and had a wooden handle. The blades weren't sharp so it took lots of strength to push it hard enough to make the blades go around, much less cut through the grass. Since Jim was the oldest boy it was generally his responsibility to keep the lawn mowed. Sometimes he made a deal of some kind with Wendy and she would do it because she was nearly as strong as he was. I wanted to push the mower but wasn't allowed to because Mama had heard terrible stories of children pushing hard and losing their grip on the handle and falling into the blades. It seemed that often there was some tale of misfortune that put a cloud over things that seemed fun but were forbidden.

After Jim cut the grass he brought Monroe out of the pasture on his halter and strutted him around the yard, practicing for the county fair which was just three weeks away. We all clapped and cheered and were Jim's pretend audience. Monroe had to learn to walk around when lots of people were watching him and not be distracted or try to jerk away. He did pretty well and Jim was proud of him. The 4-H leader came around about every week or so and put Monroe on a little scale he had in his trailer. They recorded his weight and Jim beamed at Monroe's progress.

It seemed like a long afternoon waiting for Daddy's return. Finally his truck came into the barnyard. He was alone. I ran to the back porch where I could see him walking toward the house. I was worried about what happened to Mr. Schupe. But then I heard Mr. Schupe's truck engine start and he drove away in his own truck where Daddy let him out.

I scurried into the house ahead of Daddy, not wanting to miss any bit of what he had to tell Mama. But I knew he wouldn't talk of it in front of any of us. I went to my place again on the back porch where I could listen through the screen door. They thought I was playing with the other kids. I didn't like myself for being such a sneak, but I had to know what had happened.

Daddy knew the sheriff of our county and had talked to him. Our sheriff had to get in touch with the sheriff from the county in Wyoming where Rock Springs was located. Apparently Mr. Schupe told our sheriff his story, intentionally leaving out the two most important pieces: *where* the body was and *where* the money was hidden.

Our sheriff was going to have Mr. Schupe and Daddy return to his office again the next day at which time the sheriff from Wyoming would be there to officially hear the story. Our sheriff advised Mr. Schupe to have an attorney with him. I didn't know what an attorney was except it was a person who would be on Mr. Schupe's side. Why didn't Daddy qualify? After all, he was the one who believed the story and brought Mr. Schupe to see the sheriff in the first place.

Mr. Schupe told Daddy he had a ten-year-old son named Roy whose leg was crippled by polio. An operation could strengthen his leg but it would cost several thousand dollars and they had no insurance. Roy's mother had died when he was young. Mr. Schupe had total care of his son, except for this summer after he sent Roy to live with his grandmother in Kansas. Mr. Schupe had worked long hours at a coal mine to earn money for the surgery, but was laid off. He was beside himself trying to find a way to earn money for the operation. That was when he found the money bag by the river.

The conversation between Mama and Daddy was intense and long. I heard Mama say several times she was glad Daddy was helping Mr. Schupe, but it frightened her for him to be involved in it at all, even as an innocent bystander. I agreed to myself that it was awfully scary business.

I hoped to see Sam that evening so I could tell him all the latest happenings. After supper we were playing in the yard just before dark, when I thought I heard Sam call my name. I ran into the barnyard and there he was, smiling his big friendly smile. He was on his way home for the night but wanted to tell me my herd was still doing well. He hadn't seen any bears or coyotes lately and that made me really happy. I told him about Mr. Schupe and his crippled son. I told him about all the scary things Daddy and Mama talked about. I poured it all right out.

Sam listened as he chewed on a grass stem. When I finished he asked if I was scared about any of it. I told him I was mostly worried because I wanted everyone to be okay. I wasn't afraid of robbers anymore because two were in jail and the third was dead. But I sometimes dreamed about seeing a man with a knife in his back and it woke me up. Sam assured me it was just my mind playing tricks, and that was probably why Daddy and Mama didn't want us kids to know all about it because it was too scary. He was right. Sam was always right. He patted me on the head like he always did and strode off through the dusk of evening and out of sight.

*Evie in the center with her hat surrounded by siblings.*

## 15

## TELLING THE AUTHORITIES

Daddy went again the next day with Mr. Schupe and was gone for several hours. We weeded the garden and helped Mama with her washday laundry, which took what seemed like all day to me.

Finally Mama let us go play. Most of us ran across the lane to the trees except the big girls who had better things to do and Little Larry who had to take his nap. Our tree was a mighty pirate ship that day. Wendy had made a flag with a skull drawn on it in black crayon. Jim whittled swords for us from the green shoots of the cottonwoods.

There was a little creek that ran along at the foot of the trees. Throughout the summer we made lots of makeshift bridges along it to not get wet, but it was fun when we accidentally stepped into the water. It was a playground paradise. On the days that our treehouse wasn't a pirate ship, it was Robin Hood's hideout or anything else we wanted it to be.

Late in the afternoon Mama called out the back door for Wendy and me to come and help get supper, so we left our pirate ship and swords and ran home. She already had something yummy cooking in the oven. We snapped the tips off the long green beans we picked earlier so Mama could boil them. We set the table and put on the homemade bread she had sliced, butter, a pitcher of cold milk and a pitcher of water.

The kitchen seemed extra warm on summer days when the stove was hot. Mama usually opened the windows so a cooler breeze moved through which felt so wonderful. With the kitchen windows open we could hear the birds in the trees just outside the house and the kids playing in the trees. Those familiar sounds and the homey aroma of a meal cooking and the fragrance coming in from the flowerbed are still vivid in my memory so many years later. It was a mixture of the finest things the senses could absorb and bask in.

Daddy came inside. He hung his nice hat on the peg in the back room we called the washroom. That is where Mama kept her washing machine and all sorts of things like coats, boots, hats, fly spray, and other odds and ends. He washed his hands in the bathroom sink and sat down on a wooden chair in the kitchen. He looked tired but smiled at Mama with what I interpreted to be an "everything will be okay" smile. She smiled back and busied herself. She told Wendy to call the kids for supper. Wendy had a loud voice that could carry a mile so she hollered and everyone came running.

From the oven Mama lifted her big, well-used roaster with a barbecued rib roast done to perfection. She set it on a thick pad on the table along with a bowl of fresh red potatoes from the garden and the beans Wendy and I picked and snapped. There was never a disappointment at mealtime. Daddy asked if we had all washed our hands. We waited while Mack took Little Larry back to the bathroom for a wash-up. Then we bowed our heads as Daddy offered a prayer. Mealtime was more than eating time at our house. It was together time. It was teaching and reporting time. It was a time when we sat in a circle and looked each other in the eye and bonded with each other. It seemed like the nucleus of our world.

I knew Daddy would have a mountain of information to tell Mama after supper and I could hardly wait. Daddy seemed a little more relaxed than the day before. He asked each of us different questions about what we did all day. He asked how my herd was doing and I reported that Sam said it was fine and the lambs were really big. He smiled and said his lambs were getting big too.

Since Wendy and I helped with supper, it was Kari and Lucy who did the dishes. We all helped clean things off the table. Our time in the living room that evening was cozy. The radio played soothing music while we each did our own quiet activity. Daddy and Mama took a walk together alone. That was okay on a beautiful summer night. But oh, how I wished I could be in Mama's pocket to hear the things Daddy must have told her.

When they came back they both seemed to be in a good mood. I wondered if I would ever be able to piece things together without hearing what had happened at the sheriff's office. Did Mr. Schupe tell where the dead man was? Did Daddy know? My head was filled with unanswered questions as I drifted off to sleep.

We began the next day by doing our morning chores. It wasn't until late morning that I noticed Mr. Schupe's truck just outside the barnyard. He hadn't come back with Daddy. I was so curious that I tried to find Daddy just to ask him about it. Daddy and Jim were near the pasture working with Monroe, adjusting his little halter so it would fit him better now that he had grown so much.

I asked about the truck. Daddy explained Mr. Schupe was going to stay with the sheriff for a few days and asked us to keep the truck at our place. That seemed okay except I couldn't figure out why he had to stay with the sheriff. Daddy just said there were still lots of things to figure out about what happened with the robbers, so Mr. Schupe would be in Rock

Springs for a while. It didn't occur to me that he was taken to the county jail there and held as a suspect or at least a person of interest in the investigation.

Daddy moved Mr. Schupe's truck inside the barnyard back against the fence where it was out of the way. Later that morning I heard Daddy and Mama talking about things I had never heard of—words like motive, opportunity, alibi and that type of thing. I didn't know what they were and if it was good to have them or if it was bad to have them. All I could piece together was Mr. Schupe's attorney was helping him sort out those things.

Mr. Schupe had taken Daddy and several officers to the crime scene. Sure enough, the body was exactly where he said it was. Daddy stayed in the sheriff's vehicle away from the body. There were all kinds of investigators from the coroner's office. I felt bad for Mr. Schupe and hoped he could go home soon. I hoped his son Roy was happy at his grandmother's place. It was more than I could stand to think about so I went to the trees to help the other kids build another bridge across the creek. We needed to protect our treehouse which was now a castle that might be invaded, and it needed a moat.

## 16

## LAW OF THE HARVEST

The summer days were passing fast. Monroe was getting bigger and stronger. Jim was teaching him to be led around by his halter and to stop and start when Jim pulled on the little lead rope. The corn stalks in the garden were getting tall, way over my head. Mama said we would soon be eating corn on the cob.

It was only a few days until the county fair, so the big girls were working hard on their sewing projects. Daddy brought quite a few loads of baled hay into the barnyard and put it in the barn for winter. Out in the field was a stack yard where loads of loose hay had been stacked for later use. The haystack was surrounded by a tight, high fence to keep out deer and other animals.

As we played in the trees I was able to mostly forget the heavy things that plagued my mind. But off and on my thoughts turned to the many questions I had. I wondered about Mr. Schupe's boy. I tried to imagine what it would be like to always walk with crutches. I used some sticks by the trees and made crutch-like canes and tried to walk using them. I immediately tipped over and gouged a painful wound in my forearm. Wendy, the lady of the castle, immediately washed it off with water from the moat and declared me unable to fight the next battle to protect the castle.

At supper that evening Daddy was in a lighter mood than in the past several days. We enjoyed our familiar question and answer session with lots of laughter and pleasant chit chat. Just as Mama promised, we had corn on the cob from the garden. She was quick to point out the reason it grew so well was because of our help weeding and watering and caring for the plants all summer. It seemed to taste even better knowing we helped make it grow.

She was teaching us the Law of the Harvest: "You don't get something for nothing in life. As you sow, so shall you reap."

What wisdom and teaching Mama and Daddy bestowed upon us without our even knowing it. It was so easy in that family setting to forget that not everyone was secure or surrounded by love and happiness.

The next morning Daddy was getting ready to go to the field when the phone rang. Mama called him from the back porch and he came into the house to see who it was. We heard him say "yes" and "I'll be there." When he hung up he told Mama he needed to go to Rock Springs because the sheriff had questions surrounding the Schupe case and felt Daddy could help shed some light on it. The look on Mama's face reflected what she had been saying: She didn't like him to be involved in any of it, but what else could he do? He changed from his work clothes into his go-to-town clothes and hat and left in the truck. It was more than a hundred miles away so he said he might be gone most of the day.

Of course I couldn't help worrying and feeling anxious about it. The other kids went about their work and play, but it hung heavy on my mind. Perhaps it was because I had actually met and talked to Mr. Schupe when I was lost and he was the one who helped me find my way to safety that day.

The big girls got out the ironing board and iron to press their clothing projects before the 4-H leader took them to the fair building to be judged. The judging was the day before the fair actually began. They argued over who got to be first to use the iron and ended up drawing straws from the broom. Kari won the longest straw and Lucy pouted while she waited. Mama said they hadn't learned much if they hadn't learned to share something as simple as an iron and ironing board.

She said she had plenty of other things they could iron later while they thought about it. She didn't tolerate us fighting with one another over anything. That small threat turned those two big girls into best friends again. I saw a little smile flicker on Mama's face as she turned back to the kitchen. She was a master at camouflaging correction with a simple-stated fact.

Jim didn't have to take Monroe to the fairgrounds until the next morning. He hoped Daddy wouldn't have to go back to Rock Springs again. He tied Monroe to the clothesline post as he had a dozen times or more before so he could comb his wool and wash him off and polish his little lamb hooves. When the 4-H leader came each week, they trimmed Monroe's unruly wool in various places with some little clippers so he always looked well-groomed and at the peak of perfection. They called it blocking. That was another word I didn't understand.

Soon the 4-H leader for the sewing club came and got the clothing projects Kari and Lucy worked on for several weeks. They were on wire hangers and were laid carefully on the back seat of the leader's car along with five or six outfits from other club members. Off she drove as the big girls stood and watched. They were excited but nervous to see how the judging would go. Daddy was going to help Jim take Monroe to the fair the next day when the lambs were being entered and judged. There was excitement in the air. Monroe never looked better. He had no idea he was in for a big adventure of his own.

It was rather late when Daddy returned from Rock Springs that evening. Supper was over and the dishes were done. Mama fixed a plate of food and sat with him as he ate. Mr. Schupe was still being held for more questioning. The two robbers in custody were claiming he was their partner because they didn't want to be pinned for the murder of the man by the river. That is why they told the authorities earlier that the third man had gone on to Montana or the Dakotas or somewhere. Then it was convenient to use Mr. Schupe as their third partner, especially since he knew where the money was.

Now that the authorities had the dead man, Daddy explained, they had to figure out if he was even connected at all to the robbery or if he was another case altogether. This information was too huge for me to understand. I just wanted Mr. Schupe to be okay. The law-enforcement people were doing fingerprints on the knife and trying to match them with someone. When the men fought they must have worn gloves or wiped the knife handle off because their prints weren't on it.

Of course Mr. Schupe's fingerprints weren't on the knife either. It was a big mystery. Daddy said Mr. Schupe was still being held because of something called "contempt," meaning he wouldn't say where the money was until he was sure they believed him. So things were deadlocked.

All the big words and talk of jail and robbers was not good to hear about at bedtime. Usually Daddy and Mama spoke of those things away from us where we couldn't hear. But Daddy was tired and just poured it all out to Mama. The little kids weren't in the kitchen and didn't hear any of it. The big girls were trying on peddle pusher pants in the bedroom to decide what to wear to the fair the next day. Jim and Wendy must have been out in the yard since I was the only one left in the kitchen with Mama.

Then Jim and Wendy came in the back door and Jim reminded Daddy they had to have Monroe at the fairgrounds to sign him in by ten the next morning. Daddy wearily put his hand on Jim's shoulder and assured him they would. But he reminded him that they had to arise earlier the following morning to get chores done before breakfast so they could leave right after. I doubt if Jim slept a wink that night. He probably had butterflies in his stomach about getting Monroe there looking good. His was a different reason than mine for not sleeping well. It was Ginny's turn for Mama to say her prayer by her bed that night, but it still calmed me down just to see her kneeling there. I fell asleep.

*Daddy and kids about to pile in.*

# 17

# THE COUNTY FAIR

The next morning there was hurrying and scurrying to get chores done, breakfast ready and all cleaned up. There was lots to do. Daddy and Jim got Monroe loaded by making him walk up a slanted, wide board into the bed of the truck. He would only go if Jim walked ahead of him and led him by the halter. They put a secure pen of panels around him so he couldn't fall out. After he was loaded they came back into the house so they could tell Mama good-bye and she could check to make sure Jim had a clean face and shirt and didn't look like a hillbilly.

I desperately wanted to go with Daddy and Jim, but Mama said they needed to do this alone and we would go later. The other kids were excited to go too. Mama made sure we had all our work done and had on clean clothes. We would go in the Plymouth. It was a gray sedan with a visor above the windshield. It had four doors and cloth seat covers. After driving it on dusty roads for years, the dust in the seats was stifling to us. We only used the Plymouth when all of us went to town. It wasn't that it was a fancy car, because it wasn't. It was just that most of our travel was done on the back roads going to the fields or canyons which meant the truck was used.

Most of the trips to Montpelier were done in the truck because Daddy often needed to get sacks of feed or take a tractor part to the shop or something. But when all of us needed to go to town, we crammed into the Plymouth. Going to the fair was one of those times.

Mama told us to load up. Of course the big girls dibbed riding in the front seat, but they had to hold Little Larry on their laps. In the back the rest of us sat two-deep. Mama opened the little wing windows in front to send fresh air back to us. Normally riding in the Plymouth stirred me into car-sick mode. But on the day of the fair, I had my mind riveted on other things and survived the five-mile ride without nausea.

We parked in a lot next to lots of other cars and trucks. Daddy and Mama had an agreement to meet in that parking lot at a certain time. It wasn't long before he and Jim came along. Jim was fairly bouncing with excitement as he told us Monroe was all registered and in his own little pen in the lamb barn. We would go see Monroe first, then all walk to the exhibit buildings to see how the big girls got judged on their projects. Daddy carried Little Larry and Mama held Mack's hand. The rest of us followed behind in twos like a string of ducklings.

Excited noises were all around us, especially the squeal of people on the carnival rides. The Ferris wheel rose high into the sky like a big bike tire with spokes. There were people in benches riding it. I couldn't imagine being that high up. It cost quite a bit to ride, so Daddy said we'd do something else instead. Festive music filled the air and people were milling all around. It was wonderful.

There were several long barns labeled for different animals. We entered the one for lambs. Pens lined both sides and the center walkway was graveled. Each pen had straw in the bottom and a little water trough and feeding box for hay.

Monroe was halfway down the aisle and all settled in. He was happily chewing on hay leaves when we got to him. He immediately got excited, especially with Jim and Daddy, and came over to the panel and stuck his nose out. Jim reached in his pocket and gave Monroe a little pellet to munch on. Each lamb had a poster above its pen with its name. The posters were made by 4-H members. There were all kinds of names but I thought Monroe had the best name. It sounded solid and royal.

We walked through the horse and cow barns. They even had a barn for chickens and rabbits. Each barn had its own unique odor depending on the animals. Living on a farm, I recognized each one. I could have walked through any of the barns with my eyes closed and identified the animals housed there. We walked past the place where the animals would be shown. It was a grassy little arena with a fence around it and low bleachers on two sides. There were gates on both ends. Animal showing would be the next day.

It was a time of harvest and completion. The big girls were excited to get to the 4-H exhibit building to see how they rated on their clothing projects. We walked across the grassy area with Daddy and Mama stopping to visit briefly with other men and women as they came and went. It was a time of celebration, a time to show off produce and works of art and animals. Kari and Lucy urged us on. We looked at all the tables of cooking projects, flower projects, beaded work and so forth.

At the far end on one side were the clothing projects displayed on hangers. Kari and Lucy squealed at the same time. They each won a blue ribbon—the top honor—for their work. Mama praised them, commenting they had certainly worked hard and earned it. They bumped into some of their girlfriends. Daddy said they could join their friends walking through the fair and carnival. He gave Kari and Lucy a dollar bill to share.

I suppose they just wanted to show how grown up and independent they were. Daddy told us earlier when we walked through the carnival to hold tight to someone's hand. He wasn't sure all the carnival workers were nice people all the time. He said when he was a boy a gypsy fortune teller lured someone into her tent and they were never seen again. I wasn't sure I believed it, but it made an impression on us kids.

We could smell the aroma of corn dogs and other carnival and fair-time foods. There were displays of cotton candy, caramel-coated apples and other enticing goodies. Mama and Daddy decided we could each have a corn dog and a soda pop. What a treat! We went to a shady spot on the grass and sat and waited while Daddy and Mama stood in a long line. We had a hard time keeping Mack and Little Larry from running around where we couldn't watch them. I wished that the big girls were there to help.

Daddy and Mama returned, carrying a big tray of food. We sat on the ground picnic style while Mama doled it out. It was so delicious. Even the little boys sat and ate. Some of the pop was root beer and some of it orange. That was the first time I had tasted orange soda and I made up my mind right then and there that it was my favorite flavor.

After eating we gathered up the paper packaging and paper cups and put them in a trash can. Daddy said we could each have one ride. Rides cost a dime. Jim and Wendy went on the big Ferris wheel. Ginny, Mason and Nancy rode a merry-go-round with wooden horses on poles that went up and down. I thought they were painted pretty but weren't at all like a real horse ride, so I chose not to ride on it. Mack and Little Larry rode in a little train car that went around and around on a track.

I was prone to motion sickness so I just stood next to Mama, who clapped each time they circled near. The rides all ended near the same time. We went to see Monroe one more time before going home. As we were walking back toward the barns, Little Larry threw up his corn dog on the grass. Mama got some paper out of the trash can and did her best to clean it up. I was glad I didn't go on a ride.

Monroe was happy to see us again and seemed content in his new accommodations. Jim was nervous about leaving him overnight, but Daddy reassured him the animals were safe and we would be back tomorrow. He thought Monroe was having a good time. With that, Jim relaxed.

We met the big girls in the parking lot as planned and saw they each had a new neck scarf purchased from a most handsome vendor. They giggled as they told us about it. It was one of those times Wendy and I shot a look at each other that said, "I'm so glad I'm not a teenager!" Wendy and I volunteered to ride home in the truck with Daddy and Jim. That made the Plymouth less crowded. My regret was that we couldn't ride in the back all the way home because we were on the big highway and Daddy said it was too dangerous because he had to drive fast like other cars.

Weeding awaited us in the garden at home. The sky was overcast and it was a good time to do it while it wasn't so hot. We worked the rest of the afternoon and hauled more weeds to the chickens. As we were hauling the weeds I glanced at the pasture behind the house and saw the pet lambs and thought about Monroe. I hoped he was happy with the other cute lambs at the fair barn.

That evening near supper time the sky grew dark and angry with distant claps of thunder roaring across the hills. Mama made chicken noodle soup which we all loved. As we were just sitting down to eat, the electricity went off. Daddy lit a lantern which threw enough light on the table for us to eat. The lightning and thunder got closer and closer until it was snapping around us. Then the sky opened up and torrents of rain poured down from the sky. I was glad Monroe was in a safe barn. I thought of the herds on the hills and hoped they were sheltered under some brush for protection. I was sure Sam had gone home early on this stormy night. He would have been smart enough to see the storm coming.

The power was out for most of the evening. The storm cooled the house so Mama opened the oven door of the kitchen stove, which threw out quite a bit of heat. Daddy set the lantern in the center of the kitchen table. Most of us sat around and read or drew pictures or visited. There was no radio to listen to but that was okay because we had plenty to talk about with the winning of ribbons and the adventure of going to the fair.

Monroe was given No. 7 and would be judged the next day with the other animals. Daddy kept reassuring Jim that Monroe was safe inside the fair barn. He surely was warmer and drier than if he were at home in the back pasture with other lambs getting rained on.

## 18

## MONROE'S BIG MOMENT

The first sound each morning on the farm was the roosters crowing in the barnyard. Then the birds in the trees began chirping. How I loved those sounds! The rain from the night before washed the earth and cooled it down so it was more pleasant and less dusty.

The world just seemed to be more colorful and fresh. This promised to be a very good day. The plan was much like the day before—doing chores early, then going to the fair shortly after breakfast. Everyone pitched in to help. After breakfast was all cleaned up Mama had us get ready. It meant fresh braids for Wendy, Ginny, Nancy and me. The big girls fixed their own hair and sometimes helped braid ours when Mama's hands weren't enough. Clean shirts were a must for all the boys. Jim was to look especially well-groomed and sharp because he would be showing Monroe that very day.

We all rode in the Plymouth. Daddy drove and had to take his hat off so it wouldn't hit the car ceiling. We were piled a bit deeper, but excitement compensated for the feeling of being crammed in like sardines. There was no bothersome dust anywhere because of the storm. We parked in the lot with dozens and dozens of other cars and trucks. Families were scurrying everywhere. Excitement was definitely in the air. The huge Ferris wheel was working again along with all the other rides, games and food vendors. As we walked toward the barns I scanned to see if I could see any gypsies, but I wasn't sure what to look for.

Soon we were at the lamb barn. Monroe was really happy to see Jim and Daddy, even happier than he was yesterday. His pen and the whole barn was dry inside so he must have had a good night's sleep. Jim and Daddy stayed in the barn with other 4-H kids and their dads and leaders. Mama took the rest of us to find a place on the bleachers. People were beginning to fill in the benches. The grass was still damp enough that no one wanted to sit on it until it dried out more.

A man with a clipboard and a loud voice announced it was time to start. A hush came over the seated crowd and all we could hear was the distant whine and whirr of the carnival rides. He explained the lambs had all been weighed that morning and would be given their respective ribbons as they were shown in the ring. Expectation was in the air.

As the names of the lambs and their owners were announced they were each led out into the ring. Collectively we held our breath. When Monroe and Jim were announced it was all we could do to keep from hollering. But Mama said to be polite. We clapped extra loud. Monroe looked like a million dollars and so did Jim. They marched out smartly, Monroe holding his head high. Jim was all man leading him along. Daddy stood by the fence with the other leaders and fathers.

After all the contestants were in the ring, the entire group strode around two complete times while the judges sized them up and made notations on clipboards. Each of the twenty or so lambs had a big number pinned to their back. Monroe's number was seven. Jim had a paper with a seven on it pinned to the back of his shirt.

Then the announcer told them to stop and stand still. The judges all stood together outside the ring and compared notes for a few minutes. Some of the lambs got restless, but Monroe was quiet and a perfect contestant. Two of the judges came back into the ring with a box of ribbons. The announcer called the numbers of the lambs one by one and announced their status. First they gave the white or third place ribbons. The judge pinned the ribbons on the side of their halters. Some girls with lambs cried over their white ribbon after all their hard work. I didn't blame them at all.

Then the red ribbons were given for second place. The ribbons were pinned again to the halters. Parents on the benches clapped. Then came the blue ribbons. We were excited knowing that Jim must be getting a blue because he didn't get white or red. But all the blues were given and pinned. Jim and one other boy stood with their lambs, looking rather dejected with no ribbons. The announcer called the other boy's number and the judges pinned a big pinkish ribbon on his lamb that said "Reserve Champion." I didn't know what that meant but Mama whispered that it was about the highest award. Wow! But what about Jim?

Then, to our thrill, the man pinned a big purple ribbon on No. 7 that said "CHAMPION." Boy did we clap! Monroe was the top winner! The man told contestants to take their lambs back to the pens until the fat sale, which would start in a half hour. Daddy helped Jim get Monroe back into his private pen. They hung the purple ribbon on the wood board above the pen so Monroe wouldn't get it dirty. Monroe just drank lots of water and nibbled hay leaves as though it was business as usual.

We stayed on the bleachers so we would have a place to sit for the fat sale. There were lots more people coming to watch.

Mack and Little Larry got down under the bleachers and found a few treasures before Mama could pull them back up again. The big girls helped Mama hold Little Larry when he got wiggly. Soon the man with the loud voice came back and said the sale was starting. The auctioneer, wearing a big white hat, stood near him. Some helpers brought a short ladder with a seat on top to the auctioneer. He climbed up and sat on it where he could see really well.

The lambs were invited back into the ring by their numbers so Jim and Monroe were seventh. Each time a lamb was re-introduced, the owner would walk it around the ring several times. People in the audience would increase the selling price by raising their hands as the auctioneer, talking really fast, called out the current bid. It went higher and higher until the auctioneer yelled "Sold!" Then the lamb would go back to its pen and a new lamb would come into the ring.

When they called No. 7, Jim and Monroe went around the ring a few times as numbers flew through the air. The numbers were getting bigger and bigger until the auctioneer finally yelled "Sold!" Jim and Monroe went back to the pen. A man gave Daddy a paper with the buyer's name on it.

At that point reality started to settle on Jim. He had not thought much about the fact that Monroe was going to walk out of his life that day. Daddy was there to comfort him. There were several other 4-H kids who were crying and telling their lambs good-bye. Jim got in the pen with Monroe and buried his face in his wool and sobbed like a baby. Monroe sniffed his clothing and bleated a soft sound and went on eating.

We watched in agony as Jim bade Monroe farewell. We all told him goodbye and most of us cried. It was so real and so painful. Mama said we should all go to the car except Jim and Daddy. So we did. We waited there. Our desire to see any more of the fair was gone.

Eventually Daddy and Jim came. Jim was carrying some papers and the purple ribbon and Monroe's empty halter. He sat in the front seat between Mama and Daddy. We were all rather quiet as we rode home. What was there to say? We could hear Jim's muffled sobs. Little Larry asked what was wrong with Jim and Daddy explained he felt sad and missed Monroe. That satisfied Little Larry. The rest of us were hurting too.

When we got home Mama got her wash tubs and started the big project of laundry. The big girls made sandwiches for the family for dinner. The little kids played and many of us helped Mama. No one noticed that Jim had slipped away. It wasn't until Mama called us for dinner that we saw he was gone. Everyone looked around and called and called. Wendy and I knew where he had gone. He was seeking solace in the treehouse. Mama asked us to leave him alone for a few hours and he would come home when he was ready.

He did come back a couple of hours later, all swollen-eyed and cried out. He took Monroe's halter to the shed and hung it next to the bridles and other halters. He put the big purple ribbon on the wall in the kitchen with a thumbtack where we could all see it. Mama didn't say a word about it making a hole in the wall. He put his papers in his drawer in the boys' bedroom. Jim would talk about Monroe when he was ready but we were not to mention it just yet. Mama was always so wise.

Daddy told Mama that Jim took a big step toward becoming a man that day. I wondered why growing up had to hurt so much.

*Evie on far left with brother and sisters.*

# 19

## SUMMER SUNSET IN SIGHT

We were kept busy for the rest of the day with the laundry. Hanging clothes to dry in the fresh breeze and then taking them off the line and bringing them in to put away took a long time. Eventually it was time to drain the tubs and washer and call it a good day.

I hadn't seen or talked to Sam for a few days and it seemed like there was a lot to tell him with Monroe being sold and Mr. Schupe still in the Rock Springs jail. Sam didn't seem to be around that night. I knew he was either watching my herd or he was home with his pretty wife and her big hat.

The next day Daddy planned to drive to Rock Springs to visit with Mr. Schupe and see how his case was coming along. Mama didn't want him to go since there was always so much to do around the farm to keep up with things. But she knew Daddy felt responsible to help and support Mr. Schupe the best he could. So she agreed he should go see him.

Daddy left early. He assigned Jim and Wendy to milk the cows. I was to feed the chickens and let them into their chicken run and make sure they had plenty of water. When I opened the granary door to get grain and mash for the chickens I saw a half-used bag of lamb pellets lying there. A pang of sadness over Monroe ran through me. I thought it would be hurtful if Jim were to see the bag, so I rolled the top of it over to close it tightly and placed it behind some other bags of grain where it would be out of sight.

I fed and watered the hens and let them into their run. Then I gathered the eggs and counted fifteen. Carefully I carried them in the egg basket to the house to Mama without breaking any. She praised me and said they were perfect for breakfast. I could smell the bacon cooking already. Jim and Wendy finished milking and cleaned up in time to join the rest of us for bacon and scrambled eggs and wild strawberry jam on our toast. Just seeing the jam made me think of my night alone on the mountain and I couldn't eat it. It was a long time before those memories stopped bothering me.

We played in the treehouse most of the afternoon while Little Larry was napping. Jim was less active than normal but did his best to participate and hide his loss. The big girls were excited when their leader brought their sewing projects back to our house. They modeled them for those of us who would watch. The ribbons they earned were worth a dollar and a half each and could be cashed in for the next few days at the fair office.

Jim's leader came and brought him a paper to also take to the fair office for the ribbon he won. It was worth four dollars. That seemed like a lot of money. Then Jim got a letter from the man who bought Monroe. It included a check for thirty-five dollars! Mama said he could buy school pants and shirts and put the rest in the bank for later. He was pleased with the money. But I knew he would have given it away in a second to have Monroe back.

Mama's mention of school clothes made us realize summer vacation was nearly over. We all groaned. We would have to squeeze every bit of joy and fun we could out of every day of summer that remained. But the fair was over. That was sort of the point of demarcation between summer vacation days and late summer days.

Daddy returned from Rock Springs rather late. He looked as tired as he did the last time he went. There was a new complication in Mr. Schupe's case. After the two robbers had been arrested and were in jail in Rock Springs, a gas station near there was held up and robbed. The thief hadn't been found and there was no way to identify him because he wore a mask.

The law officers were pointing a finger at Mr. Schupe. Mama asked Daddy when the gas station was robbed. He said it was the very night or early morning when I was lost. My heart jumped into my throat and began pounding. I knew Mr. Schupe wasn't in the Rock Springs area because I had seen him early that morning in the trees. But I promised not to tell. Would Mr. Schupe want me to talk about it now? I kept still.

Before I went to bed that night I took the blue button out of my drawer and fingered it. I thought of Mr. Schupe and his son Roy with the crippled leg. If I told Daddy and Mama about seeing Mr. Schupe that same morning would they believe me? After all, I was the one who had what they called an "imaginary" sheep herder for a friend. Sam was real to me even if he wasn't to anybody else. But maybe they would think I made up the story of seeing Mr. Schupe too. I was in a real fix. It was my turn to have Mama say her prayer by my bed that night and I was glad because it always brought me comfort. Even though she was probably not praying silently about Mr. Schupe, I was. I fell asleep while Mama was praying.

I was quiet at breakfast the next morning. As Daddy went around the table asking us questions he paused as he came to me. "How's your herd, Evie?" I said they were fine but I hadn't seen Sam since the fair. He asked if I was getting ready to sell my lambs because it was about time to talk to Slim and Beatrice and get his own lambs ready to sell. That gave me something new to think about and helped get my mind off Mr. Schupe.

*Charlie the mule ready for work.*

## 20

## EYEWITNESS

When Daddy was walking to the barnyard after breakfast I ran to catch up with him. I told him I had something to talk to him about. He took my hand in his big calloused hand and we walked over near the barn where there were bales of hay waiting to be stacked inside. We sat down together on one and Daddy looked at me.

I almost ran back to the house, but I knew I was the only one who could help Mr. Schupe. I asked Daddy if it was okay to break a promise if it meant helping someone else. He said it probably was. I told him about the morning in the trees when I met Mr. Schupe. If it was the same morning of the gas station robbery then Mr. Schupe couldn't have done it. Daddy took his hat off and looked at me in disbelief. He asked if I was sure that was the man I saw and did I really see him? I knew *exactly* what he meant about *if* I really saw him. I started to cry because it seemed like that's what I always did when the world seemed too big or too hard to deal with. Daddy wiped my cheeks with his thumb and calmed me down. He said we should go talk to Mama about it.

We walked back to the house together, holding hands, and went in the back door. Mama joined us and we sat down by the table. The other kids were elsewhere. Daddy told Mama that I had seen Mr. Schupe in the trees the morning I was lost and that I could probably help his case. She really didn't want me involved in any of the robbery mess. It was bad enough for

Daddy to be involved, and now one of her little kids would be too! They talked about it for a few minutes and decided they should take me to Rock Springs to tell the sheriff what I had seen. I said I wouldn't go unless Mama went too. She agreed.

The big girls were to take care of the family for the day while Daddy, Mama and I went to Rock Springs. Mama braided my hair and put a ribbon on the bottom of each braid. We put on our go-to-town clothes and got in Daddy's truck. It was a long ride. I had never been that far away from home before. There were a lot of cars going up and down the streets, and lots of stores and people and a park with green grass where some kids were swinging. We parked by a brick building. Daddy went in first to talk to the sheriff as Mama and I waited in the truck. She dampened a corner of a handkerchief and wiped one of my ears. I thought I had washed up good, but I guess not quite good enough to pass Mama's inspection.

Pretty soon Daddy came out and opened the truck door for Mama and me to get out. He winked at me so I trusted everything would be okay, but I held tight to Mama's hand. We walked up many steps and Daddy pushed the big glass door open for us. The wooden floor creaked as we walked across it toward the sheriff's office. He stood and shook hands with Mama and smiled at me. The three of them talked while my eyes darted around the room, looking at a big rack of rifles with a glass door on it and a big lock. There were pictures of scary-looking men and a few women tacked to a bulletin board. I thought the room smelled like wood oil the way school floors smelled after they have been oiled.

Mr. Schupe had told the sheriff he was in the forest on the morning in question and he had talked to a little girl. We learned he was an Army veteran and a loner by nature.

After losing his coal-mining job he had been sleeping in his pickup and mostly fishing and living off the land when he came upon the three robbers and their stolen loot.

The pieces of the puzzle were slowly coming together, at least this part of the puzzle. I told the sheriff my story, without actually looking at him. Then he had me sit in a chair by the desk and look at pictures of faces in a book. All I had to do was point to the man I had seen in the trees. The chair was too low so I sat on Mama's lap.

I looked at lots of pictures until I thought they all looked quite a bit alike. Then I saw him! In an instant I recognized Mr. Schupe's face. I moved my finger across the page of pictures. It moved like a needle on a thermostat, slowly, slowly until it reached Mr. Schupe's face. Then I stopped and looked up at the sheriff. He smiled until it made his mustache curl up. "Are you sure?" he asked.

I nodded my head up and down without taking my eyes off his mustache. He said it would certainly help clear things up for Mr. Schupe as far as the gas station holdup. Mama and I went back to the truck. But first we drank from a white porcelain water fountain. A little bubble of water came straight up in the center on a bulb-like thing with a hole in it. Mama said to not let my lips touch the fountain. Daddy stayed in the building and talked to the sheriff and Mr. Schupe a little longer. When we got in the truck Mama said I did a really good thing and she was proud of me. I was happy.

Daddy drove to a hamburger stand and a big girl like Kari or Lucy came out to the truck. Daddy told her we wanted three hamburgers and three drinks, two root beers and one orange soda. He recalled how much I loved orange soda on fair day. I was amazed Daddy and Mama could remember so much about each of us individually when they had ten kids to take care of, but they did.

Soon the girl came back and hooked a little tray to Daddy's window. Sure enough, the hamburgers and drinks were right. Daddy gave the girl some money and handed us our food. We put our drinks on the wide, flat dashboard. Daddy and Mama talked about all sorts of things. I watched the girl go back and forth to other cars and take food. Daddy said she was called a "car hop," but I only saw her walk. She was chewing gum and her hair was pulled back in a ponytail. I thought if Kari and Lucy knew her they would like her.

*Daddy's flock.*

## 21

## TRAILING, SELLING SHEEP

It had been a busy few days and I was tired, so I laid my head on Mama's lap and fell asleep as we drove home. The next thing I knew we were pulling into our barnyard.

Most of the kids had been playing in the trees and came running to greet us. The big girls were in the house listening to music so they could keep an eye on Little Larry while he took his nap. I was glad to be home. It seemed like a refuge from all the unpleasant problems of the big world. I told Jim and Wendy about the sheriff with the mustache and the white drinking fountain. They seemed impressed. They asked if I wanted to go on the pirate ship with them because they found a treasure and were taking it away to an island to bury it. I ran with them to the trees.

After supper that night Mama announced we would be weeding the garden in the morning and she expected lots of help. Daddy would be going to town for supplies for Slim and Beatrice and would be going to their camp the day after. There was lots to do and lots to look forward to. We all knew that with summer vacation winding down we needed to take advantage of all the things we could.

I saw Sam by the back porch just before dark and told him all of the things that happened in the last few days. As always, he listened without interrupting. He said it was getting close to time to sell the lambs and wondered if I wanted to sell mine soon. I told him he could sell them when Daddy sold his, but the mother ewes were to stay. He agreed and said the lambs were getting nearly as big as their mothers because it was such a good summer for grass. Mary was waiting for him at home so he walked toward the barnyard and was gone.

The soil was still soft from the recent deluge of rain, so pulling weeds was not hard as much as it was just tedious. Some of the weeds were getting long roots and prickly tops as they do in late summer so we wore gloves to protect our hands. The chickens were happy for the weeds. We also threw some to the horses in the back pasture. I missed seeing Monroe when we went to the lamb pasture behind the house. I knew Jim missed him terribly, but Mama said not to mention it, so we all kept mum.

We did such a good job of weeding that Mama let us have an outdoor lunch. The big girls made sandwiches and Mama helped them make lemonade and deviled eggs. We washed the soil from our hands and arms and Mama spread a quilt and tablecloth under the apple tree in the front yard in the shade. It was so fun to eat in the open air. Little Larry kept walking on the table cloth and Mama had to keep sitting him down. We ate until there wasn't even one egg, one sandwich, or a drop of lemonade left. Food always tasted so good outdoors. Wendy and I figured the best part was that there weren't many dishes to wash because it was our turn.

When Daddy came back from town he had salt for the sheep and groceries for Slim and Beatrice as well as groceries for us. He carried the boxes of food into the house and left the salt in the back of the truck. Mama put her groceries in the cupboard as he unloaded the box. He sorted what would go in the pack saddles and what would stay at our place. We hung around the table hoping he had bought a big chocolate bar or some other treat as he often did.

Just when the big box seemed almost empty he made a deep reach and came up with a sack of licorice—black, brown and red. He passed the sack around and we each got to pick the flavor of our choice. Jim convinced me black was the best so I chose a long black piece. At first it seemed nasty and not like candy at all. But Jim said if I sucked on it then it would taste sweet. He seemed to know best about most things in my world, so that's what I did. It did taste better all the time. We laughed when we looked in the bathroom mirror and saw our stained black teeth.

The plans for going to the sheep camp were the same as always. We would do our chores early and then start out right after breakfast. Daddy offered the big girls a chance to go, but they complained it was too hot. They always had a good excuse for not wanting to go. So our usual crew of Wendy, Jim and I were Daddy's helpers. The younger kids stayed home to play. Mama wasn't keen on having them gone all day on horses when she wasn't around with them.

Daddy put the pack bags in the truck and saddled Red Wing, Pomp and Charlie. The three of us rode in the back as usual.

As we left the barnyard we could see Mr. Schupe's truck still parked back by the fence. I wondered how long it would be before he could prove his innocence and get the reward money to help his crippled son.

When we got to Sage Canyon we drove up to the cabin. Mr. Leewood came out on the porch to talk to Daddy while he was loading the pack saddle bags on Charlie. He said his job with the farmer west of town had ended so they would likely be moving along in the next few days. They had begun to pack some of their things into the back of their old truck. Daddy seemed pleased they were going to move along even though they were nice. He told Mama weeks ago it was a liability concern having people live there. I didn't know what that meant, but like all the other times I didn't understand what big words meant, I trusted that Daddy always knew best.

We rode along the trail the way we always did. We could see the season was changing. The long grasses now had ripened heads of seeds and much of the grass was drier. The air was much cooler in the shady spots as we moved along. It had a different feel to it, yet it was breathtakingly beautiful. The fresh air and fragrance of the forest was constant. The animals plodded along matter of factly. In the sunny places the horse flies buzzed around us and we swatted as much as the horses did. We visited some, but mostly just rode and enjoyed the sounds and sights of the canyon. How I loved those trail rides!

When we got to camp I noticed the shady part of the clearing extended farther north which meant the sun was slowly making its seasonal change toward the south. The sun still fell on the big tent, however. No one seemed to be around so Daddy led Charlie over to the tent and started to unloosen one of the pack bags so he could unload the supplies. Jim helped him while Wendy and I tied up Red Wing and Pomp where they could eat the tall grass on the edge of the clearing. Daddy left the bags of salt in the other pack on Charlie's back.

We heard horses coming in on the trail at the back of the clearing. Sure enough it was Slim and Beatrice. They were pleased to see us. They quickly unsaddled one of their horses and put hobbles on him so he could eat and stay close around camp. The other horse was tied to a bush. Beatrice was ever the hostess at her campfire and tent. She took as much pride in the role as the lady of a castle. She insisted on feeding us while they talked business. Daddy discouraged us from gobbling up their supplies since everything had to be packed in but said we could eat oatmeal with them. It tasted almost as good as the day Beatrice fed me breakfast when I had been lost. I was always amazed at how tastes and smells triggered memories just as much as seeing things did.

The three adults talked of selling the lambs and other things. Then Daddy, Slim and Jim rode up to the salt troughs and water hole. Daddy understood a little Spanish and Slim understood a bit of English so I guess they got by. It was obvious where they were going and why, so there really wasn't much to discuss. Wendy and I helped Beatrice clean the bowls in the spring as we did before. She invited us into the tent to show us something she had been working on. It was a large afghan she had been knitting for the whole summer. She knitted while they rested in the middle of the day. It was made of bright colors with a Southwest flair.

I was astounded that something so pretty could have been created in those circumstances, but I learned through the whole summer that Beatrice had a soft and wonderful side to her nature. She had brought the yarn with her when they came but was almost out and she didn't feel like she could ask Daddy to bring yarn to her. Wendy and I had a good time listening to Beatrice's interesting tales.

When the others got back into camp about an hour later the three adults sat in the shade on blocks of wood and talked about trailing the herd down to the stockyards in town. At that point the lambs would be separated from the others and sold. They would be loaded on rail cars at the stockyards and sent to Omaha, Nebraska. Then the crew would trail the rest of the herd back up the canyon. It was eight miles from where the herd was to the stockyards. It would take one day down and one day back. I heard Daddy say he had four hundred lambs.

I figured my herd had one hundred. I didn't really know what the big numbers meant except that one was smaller than four. One hundred was a good number for my lambs. I knew Sam would keep track of it all. He would probably sell them the same day as Daddy sold his. Daddy would hire five more men to trail the sheep for the two days. They had to know how to trail sheep through traffic. It seemed like a huge undertaking, but Daddy did it every year. It wasn't until that year when I had a herd of my own that I became aware of all that had to be done. But I knew Sam would take care of everything for my herd.

Beatrice interpreted all this to her Honey Slim. Daddy would return to the canyon in one week to give them details after he talked to the buyers and set a date with them. He also had to arrange for the stockyards ahead of time.

On the way back down the trail we asked Daddy if we could help drive the herd to the stockyards. He said it would still be a week or two away and we would probably be in school. School! Was the summer vacation really almost over? We knew it was, but we didn't want it to end.

# 22

## THE SEARCH WARRANT

When we got near the bottom of the canyon we heard a commotion. As the cabin came into sight we saw several sheriff vehicles in addition to the Leewoods' truck and Daddy's truck.

Daddy was quite taken aback. We tied our horses to the brush a little ways away. Daddy told Wendy, Jim and me to stay by the horses until we knew what was happening. He walked down to the cabin. We couldn't hear what was said, so we sneaked a little closer through the bushes. We positioned ourselves across the dirt road from the cabin, close enough to hear and see.

I recognized the sheriff with the mustache. Three other men in uniforms were next to him. They all had guns strapped to their belts. There were three or four other men standing back a little bit. Their uniforms were a different shade of brown. The sheriff shook Daddy's hand. I took that as a good sign they weren't going to shoot Daddy. The sheriff with the mustache gave Daddy a paper to read. Daddy unfolded it and handed it back. They called it a search warrant and wanted to look inside the cabin. Mr. Schupe had told the sheriff the money was hidden under the floorboards. If they looked they would find it, he said.

Daddy gave his permission. The Leewoods were outside putting the last of their belongings in their truck and ready to leave, but the sheriff told them to wait. Besides there was a sheriff truck parked behind their truck and Daddy's truck. No one was going anywhere soon.

Wendy's eyes grew big when she felt a sneeze coming on and muffled it in the crook of her arm. Sagebrush always made her sneeze, especially if she was in the middle of it. No one looked up. The Leewoods were still standing by their truck. Daddy opened the door to the cabin and let two or three officers in. They had hammers and a nail puller with a long handle. We could hear the creak of the nails as they were pried loose. We couldn't see much of anything. It seemed like they pried lots of nails and boards up. We could hear the pounding as boards were replaced and the nails hammered back into them.

The men came back out of the cabin. The sheriff had two men crawl under the cabin from the outside and we froze, hoping they wouldn't see us. I thought that must be creepy with all those spiders under there, but I supposed any man brave enough to carry a gun must be brave enough to face spiders. Soon the men crawled back out from under the cabin and brushed themselves off. They shook their heads saying there was nothing there.

The sheriff walked over to the Leewoods and asked if they had seen anything suspicious while they were staying there. Mr. Leewood assured him they hadn't. Daddy said they were good guests and had taken care of the property. The sheriff asked if his men could search Mr. Leewood's truck and belongings. Mr. Leewood stiffened a bit and said that would be an invasion of his privacy. The sheriff said that since Mr. Leewood had been staying in the cabin there was probable cause to look at his things too.

The sheriff nodded his head and two of his deputies jumped up into the bed of the pickup and started to look through things. They were pretty nice and didn't rip things apart. They asked Mr. Leewood what was in the two locked bags. He told them it was his scissor samples because he was a scissor salesman by trade. The sheriff asked him to unlock the cases. Mr. Leewood took the cases out of the truck, fumbled around with his ring of keys and unlocked them both.

They were lined with black velvet and each had pairs of scissors attached to the sides. There were scissors of every size and length imaginable. The deputies finished looking inside the scissor cases and Mr. Leewood was about to close them. Then one of the deputies said he thought he saw something and to hold on for a minute. He gave a slight tug to the velvet lining and the inside wall of the case fell down, revealing packets and packets of paper money! They took the lining out of both cases and found that they were jam packed with the stolen money. Our eyes about popped out of our heads!

All the sheriffs and deputies gathered around Mr. Leewood's truck. Mrs. Leewood sat on the running board, put her face in her hands and began to cry. Slowly it dawned on everyone what happened. Mr. Schupe had hidden the money under the loose boards, and the Leewoods found it and stashed it in their scissor cases. The sheriff nodded to one of the deputies who put handcuffs on Mr. Leewood. Daddy asked if that was really necessary. He asked them to consider that Mr. Leewood just happened to find the money, was down on his luck and used poor judgment in taking it.

What a predicament. Ten minutes later and the Leewoods would have been long gone on their way to Oregon. So here was the money from the bank robbery, now found by two separate innocent men, Mr. Schupe and Mr. Leewood, who each had plans for it. The local sheriff said Mr. Leewood had to go to the station with him until things were cleared up.

Daddy invited Mrs. Leewood to come to our house to stay or she could stay in the cabin. She chose to stay in the cabin. Daddy helped unload a few things for her from the truck. The officers took Mr. Leewood and the two scissor cases with them and drove away. Wendy, Jim and I hurried back to the horses and sat on the ground trying to figure it all out.

Daddy tied the horses behind the truck. Before we left he went back up on the porch and knocked on the door. Mrs. Leewood opened it, wiping her eyes. Daddy told her he would come back tomorrow to check on her. He said if she got worried she could drive to our house and gave her directions, but she said she didn't drive. So again Daddy said he would go back the next day to check in on her. She thanked him and we left.

As the horses clip-clopped along behind the truck, the three of us had quite a discussion about the things we had just seen. It was like a tale from a book. We felt bad for the Leewoods and decided if we ever found lots of money we would be tempted to hide it and keep it too. We talked about Mr. Schupe. He didn't want the stolen money, he just wanted the reward for finding it. He wanted it for a good reason. Jim said maybe the Leewoods had a good reason too. Maybe they had something as important in their lives as Mr. Schupe's crippled son. It was enough to make my head spin.

We got home and took care of the horses. Then, not even waiting to watch Charlie roll, we raced to the house to hear every word of what Daddy would be telling Mama. We three kids washed up and sat in the kitchen to hear what was being said. It actually felt good to me, like a big relief, to have Jim and Wendy in on some of the scary things too. I didn't like it when I had to carry the burden in my heart all alone and not talk to anyone about it. That is, no one except Sam.

Daddy hardly knew where to begin. He started at the moment when we came around the bend in the trail and saw all the activity at the cabin. Mama listened, astonished and maybe not believing everything he told. But we knew it was all true. We witnessed it through the bushes at eyeball level. Mama finally had to sit down. It was too much, too scary and too real. She said she shouldn't have let us kids go, but Daddy assured her we were way off by the horses in a safe place the whole time. Wendy, Jim and I looked at each other with our lips sewn shut.

The next day Mama rode with Daddy out to check on Mrs. Leewood. We took that as an official un-invite for us. That was okay too, since we had seen all we could understand for now. Besides, there probably wouldn't be much going on out there anyway with Mr. Leewood gone trying to clear things up.

*Shearing time.*

# 23

# FINAL PUZZLE PIECES

That evening before bedtime I got the blue button out of my drawer. I looked it over and relived the events that had led up to today. Who would have ever thought nice Mr. Leewood would end up in a bad place in the mystery?

Before putting the button back in the drawer I figured out how Mr. Schupe must have lost it, hurrying to hide the money in a deserted cabin in the middle of nowhere. But then the Leewoods moved in and we were coming and going often on the cabin trail. It wasn't in the middle of nowhere as he thought and wasn't a good hiding place after all. He must have spent lots of time hiding in the bushes for weeks, waiting for the Leewoods to move out. That's why he was in the mountains on the morning I was lost. Now the pieces were starting to fit together like a puzzle.

We did our chores and after breakfast Jim mowed the lawn while Wendy and I cleaned the living room. We swept and dusted and put everything in its place. Mama suggested we cut some flowers from her flowerbed and make two bouquets, one for the kitchen table and one for the little stand in the living room. We were generous with the flowers and had to use two of Mama's quart canning jars for vases. They looked pretty and smelled good too.

Daddy and Mama took Mack and Little Larry with them to the cabin. The big girls stayed in the house to sort through their clothes and decide what they could wear to school. The rest of us headed for the trees across the lane. I noticed the leaves weren't as green, they were beginning to be flecked with yellow. We rode in the pirate ship and searched for treasure in a field nearby—a desert island. Of course we had our swords with us for protection at all times.

When we came back to the trees we washed our tired, hot feet in the creek. Ginny, Mason and Nancy were the bridge builders and made one the day before while we were on the trail ride. Jim said it was as good as if he had built it himself and spat into the creek for emphasis. Whenever he spit we knew he meant business.

The big girls called for us to come home for lunch, so we ran like a herd of wild buffalo across the lane and into the back door. We fought over who got to wash first. Soon we were all obediently seated at our places. It seemed strange with Daddy and Mama and the two little boys gone. Kari assumed her position as the oldest and sat in Daddy's chair. Lucy followed suit and sat in the second position of authority in Mama's place. We were okay with it. We just wanted to eat. They made cold beef sandwiches because Mama didn't want us to have a fire in the stove while they were gone. We ate bottled peaches with the sandwiches. They were delicious. Then, before the big girls could assign us clean-up duty, we headed back to the trees.

After a while we heard the truck coming so we ran home into the barnyard just as it pulled in. Little Larry had fallen asleep so Daddy carried him into the boys' room and laid him on his bed. Mama pulled his blankie up around him. When we asked how Mrs. Leewood was, they said she was fine. But I think there are all degrees of fine. Sometimes it means you are happy and things are really okay. Sometimes it means you are just surviving but you will keep breathing for now. I thought that must be how she really felt.

They didn't talk about it at all while we were around that afternoon, so I figured they must have discussed it on the way home until there was nothing left to tell. Daddy made phone calls to the stockyards and to some men he hired for two days to help move the herd and sell the lambs. He also called the man who would buy the lambs. They agreed to meet in town later that day. Daddy seemed nervous, but in a happy sort of way, the way Jim was the day of the fat sale...but *before* the sale. Daddy put on his best hat and left in his truck. We hurried back to the trees before Mama found work for us.

We played for quite a long time and were making bows and arrows to fortify the castle when we started smelling supper cooking. Soon we heard Mama call out the back door that Wendy and I were to come and pull carrots so she could cook them. We reluctantly left our castle and went home. We pulled carrots, careful to thin them and not just take one big clump. We washed them in the hose by the back door. Wendy got a big metal bowl and a long sharp kitchen knife. She cut the tops off and we put the clean carrots in the bowl. While she took the carrots and knife to Mama, I carried the tops to the pasture and put them over the fence for the horses. They saw me and came right over to accept my treat.

By the time Daddy got back home we had the table set for supper. Mama made fried steaks, potatoes, gravy and fresh carrots from the garden. She sliced thick pieces of bread while we filled the glasses with cold water. Soon we were all gathered around in our assigned seats. Even Little Larry was awake and in place. Daddy said the prayer as he often did. On this evening he gave thanks for our family and our home and prayed for blessings on those who didn't have a home or whose families had big problems. I knew he meant the Leewoods and Mr. Schupe. I was so glad for our family.

Daddy made a deal to sell the lambs at the best price he had gotten in years. The way Slim and Beatrice talked, the lambs were as big as any they had seen, with fewer coyote losses. Daddy said it should be a good year when things were settled. We were eating when we noticed Mama wiping her eyes. No one dared to say a word. Daddy asked if she was all right. She pretended to get something over by the sink and wiped her eyes and then came back and sat down. Again Daddy asked. She said she just felt so bad for Mrs. Leewood, up the canyon all alone and her husband in jail and in trouble. I think Daddy's prayer had reminded her of the blessings we were enjoying together and she couldn't stand to think of deep sorrow in other people's lives.

Our conversation turned to how many days until school started. It was almost painful to know it was only about ten days away. When some of us moaned, Mama assured us life would still go on, we would just have one more big thing added to it. She said she would take some of us to Montpelier the next day to buy a few new items to wear. The big girls were happy about that. Most of us dreaded that type of shopping.

The thing I disliked most about school was having to wear a dress every day. I liked wearing pants so I could run wild and play hard. Acting quiet like a "little lady" just wasn't in my nature. But maybe if I got some nice new socks and a pair of shoes without a hole in the bottom I would be happy to go shopping. It also meant Jim and Mason would need a haircut.

Maybe Mama would even trim the girls' hair a bit. It had grown during the last three months of summer. There was much to do. We took baths that night and Mama checked us for ticks. Fortunately there were none to report. I started to think it might be fun to go to town tomorrow. I dreamed about new shoes.

Next morning after we cleaned up from breakfast and did our chores, we got ready to go to town. It meant new braids for us four younger girls. Mama had the big girls help braid. Daddy had other things to do, so Mama and all ten of us kids loaded into the Plymouth—two deep—and away we went. Mama let me ride in the front because she knew I got car sick easily. Kari was also in front holding Little Larry.

First we stopped at the shoe store. Mama told us to sit down and not move. Kari and Lucy were to keep track of Little Larry. A man with black shiny hair came and sat on a little stool in front of us. One by one he had us put a foot up on his stool so he could measure it on a long metal ruler. Then he went to a back room behind a curtain and brought out a pair of shoes in just our size. He did that over and over until we had each picked a pair of shoes that fit us and that we liked. Mama looked at the price on the end of the boxes to make sure she liked them too.

Little Larry and Mack didn't need new shoes and didn't care. They were too little to go to school anyway. Mama took some money from her purse and paid the man. Then we went to the car and Mama opened the trunk and put in eight shoe boxes with eight new pairs of shoes. Again the big girls were to hold onto Mack and Little Larry. Mama first took Jim and Mason and picked out pants for them. Jim brought a few dollars he earned from selling Monroe. He paid for his own clothes, except the shoes. Mama said she was proud of him. If we had been at home I think he would have spit and ground it into the dirt.

Then while the bigger kids sat in some red chairs with silver chrome handles by the door, she took Wendy, Ginny, Nancy and me to the dress rack and had us look at some girl's dresses. She let us each pick the dress we liked in our size. That was fairly easy. She also let us pick two new pairs of anklets and some underwear in the girl's department. It was time for Wendy and Jim to hold onto Little Larry while the big girls shopped. Our purchases were wrapped in brown paper with a string tied around them. It made quite a pile of goods.

Kari and Luci didn't want to buy anything without trying it on first, so it took a long time. They each got a dress and accessories. Mama said with their 4-H projects and fixing last year's clothes they should have enough to start school. Maybe they could sew or buy more later. I had had enough shopping to last a lifetime. Mama opened the trunk again and we put our packages inside. Kari and Luci made sure theirs were on top where they wouldn't get wrinkles. Wendy and I rolled our eyes at that.

It was hot and we begged Mama to buy us soda pop somewhere, but she said she had spent too much money already and that when we got home she would make lemonade. We each carried our own packages into the house. Mama told us to put the dresses on hangers so they wouldn't wrinkle. I was actually pretty happy with my new shoes. They were black and white saddle oxfords.  I wanted to put them on to see how fast I could run in them, but Mama said to wait.

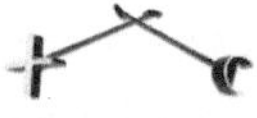

# 24

## LAST TRAIL RIDE

While we were in town shopping Daddy had some visitors—the sheriff from Rock Springs and our county sheriff. They had Mr. Leewood with them as well as Mr. Schupe.

Mr. Schupe had been cleared because all the money from the bank robbery was found and he had led the sheriff to the crime scene where the other two robbers had murdered their partner. Mr. Schupe's story checked out and he would receive the five-thousand-dollar reward as he had hoped. When we got home Mr. Schupe's truck was gone. He was headed to Kansas to get his son Roy and arrange for his leg surgery.

Mr. Leewood was released because everything else checked out and he had turned the money over to the sheriff. Daddy had driven Mr. Leewood back to the cabin, much to the relief of Mrs. Leewood. He was fined fifty dollars for being in possession of the money without reporting it. That was all he had earned working for the farmer west of town. Otherwise the judge was lenient and let him go. Daddy suggested Mr. Leewood stay a few more days so he could earn money helping Daddy trail the sheep. Mr. Leewood agreed and Mrs. Leewood was weak with relief.

I wished I could see Mr. Schupe again. I wanted to know where he had been sleeping and what he had been eating all the time since I saw him that first day on the trail ride. I was also hoping to see if he had a happy face this time. Daddy said

Mr. Schupe had been going back and forth to town for food and supplies and had mostly slept in his truck. Now all those hard days were worth it. Daddy assured me he was smiling a lot as he left, which made me happy.

That night after supper I had a long talk with Sam by the back porch. I had so many things to tell him. He knew everything was going to be okay the whole time. He said he would return when he could to see me. But now that summer was almost over, he wouldn't be around quite as much because he would be busy selling lambs and things like that. He reminded me that I would be busy too. Before he left he told me to be happy.

The thistle tops had turned from purple to white and combines had begun cutting grain in the fields. The leaves had turned completely yellow. There were flocks of birds forming V-shapes in the sky as they headed south. Each day the air was cooler. There was a kind of sadness inside me as I watched summer slipping away one day at a time. It had been such a wonderful summer, filled with many kinds of adventures. New people to meet, mysteries to solve, obstacles to overcome and losses to endure. There had been laughter and tears, happiness and fears. It had been a time of growth for each of us.

We learned how blessed we were each day as we sat as a whole family at our dinner table. We knew that many others weren't so fortunate. We had all grown an inch or two on the outside and more than that on the inside. I didn't see Sam as often after that week.

When I was alone I sat in the treehouse and watched the clouds float by and was glad for this summer—the summer of the herds, my seventh summer—a summer I would never ever forget.

## ALL ABOUT EVE

Eve was born February 3, 1947, to William Butterfield Crane and Lula Robison Crane. She became the fifth of ten children and grew up on the family farm in Bennington, near Montpelier, Idaho where she was taught to work and to cherish family values. Eve attended elementary school in Bennington and Georgetown and Lincoln Junior High in Montpelier. After graduating from Montpelier High School in 1965, she earned an associate of arts degree in journalism from Ricks College, Rexburg, Idaho.. In 1968 she was a nanny in Honolulu, Hawaii for several months. The following year Eve took communication classes at Penn State University.

Writing was Eve's favorite hobby. She wrote for the *Viking Scroll* at Ricks College and had articles printed in the *Idaho Falls Post Register* and the *Rexburg Standard Journal*. She also wrote for the *News Examiner* in Montpelier and had a column, "Poet's Nook." She was one of the original "Pescadero Poets," a club of Bennington women who wrote and shared a poem each month, published in a yearly collection. Eve wrote several scripts for church productions, co-authoring "On the Bethlehem Road." She was employed by Dr. Paul H. Daines as office manager for over ten years, then worked at Agrium, Inc. as a payroll clerk and secretary. After retiring from Agrium she returned to work for Dr. Daines as a bookkeeper and personal assistant.

She married Mark Taylor Dayton on March 24, 1971. They lived and raised their family in Bennington. Eve was involved in community and church service throughout her life. She loved the Gospel of Jesus Christ and had a deep understanding of the scriptures, often shared with others.

Eve was known for her wit, being the life of the party, and for her wide range of knowledge. She was a grand storyteller with a zest for life; enjoying the outdoors, reading, raising "bum" lambs, fishing with her kids and grandkids, and of course, writing. In recent years she wrote several novels. Her devotion and greatest purpose in life was to her family who adored her.

Eve passed away from cancer on August 28, 2022.

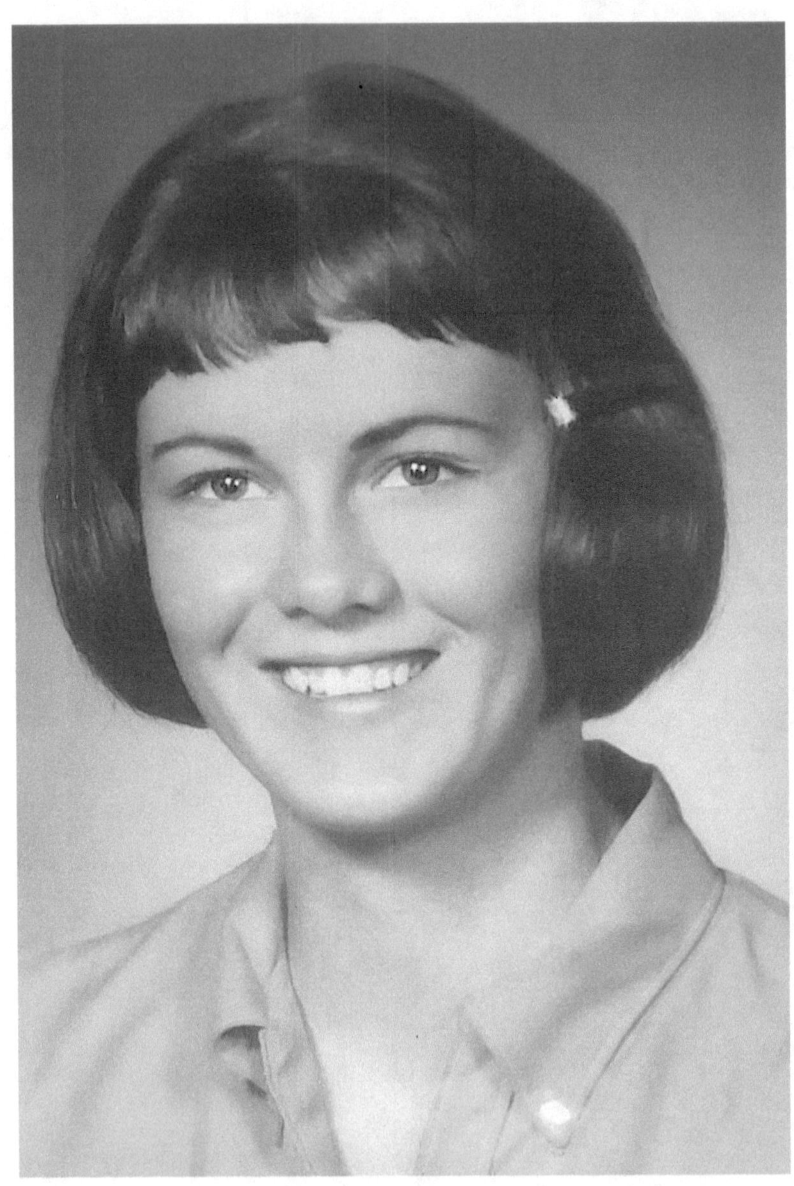

*Eve Idella Crane, age 19.*

*Mark and Eve Dayton family.*

*(l to r) Reed & Courtney Crane, Benjamin & Cindy Bishop, Mark & Eve, Brad & Cathy Martin, Chad & Rachel Eberhardt.*

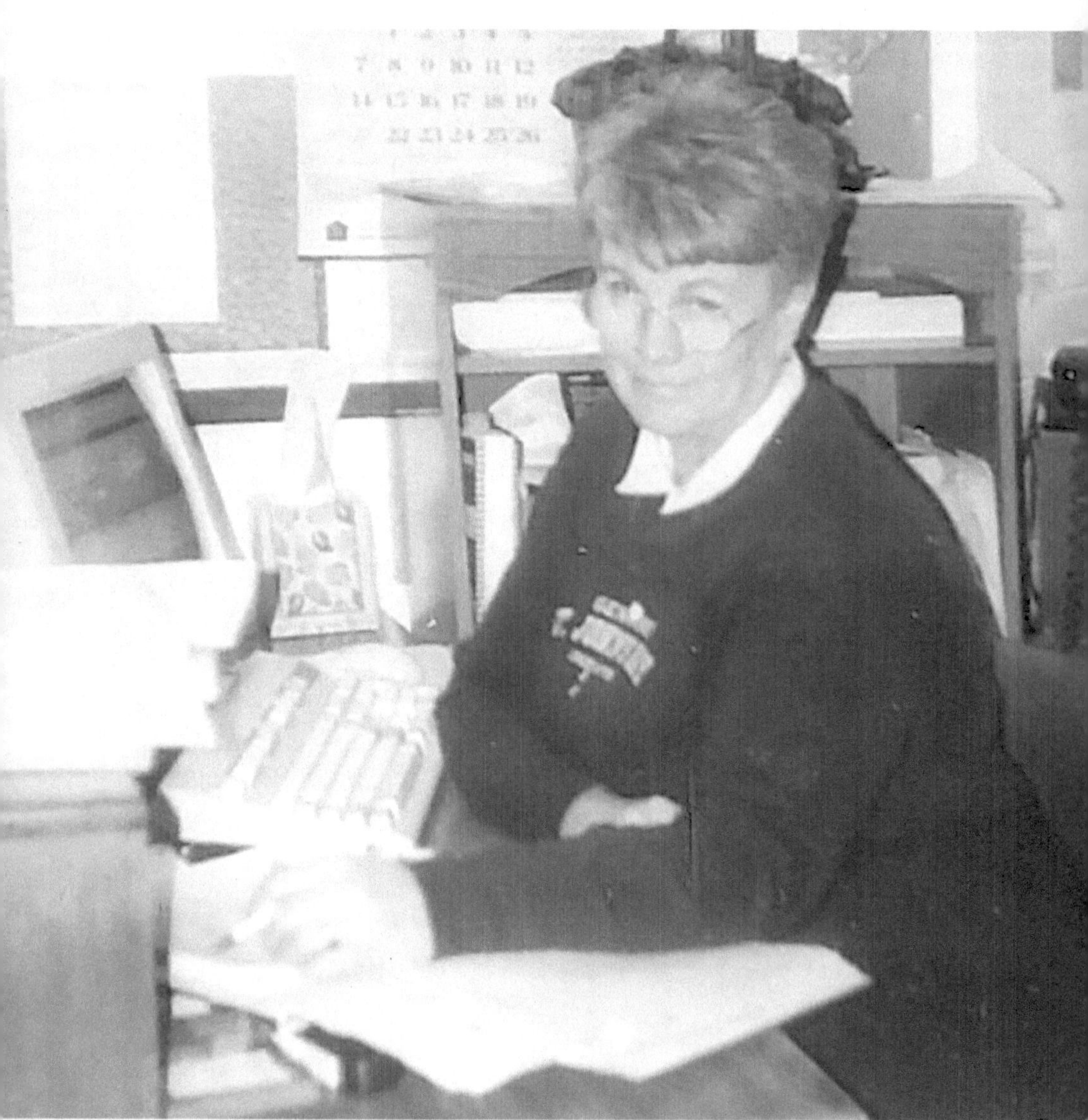

*The author at work.*

*Grandchildren on Eve's beloved bridge.*

# AFTERWORD

by
Vicki Cochran Smith

*Farm girl and friend who joined Eve's Montpelier High School group in the 1960s*

I miss the sights and smells and incredible sense of security growing up in rural southeastern Idaho provided me. I loved the vistas of open space with the peaceful scene of cattle grazing, the orderliness of crops being planted and harvested, and the seasons bringing all senses into sharper awareness—not only through hands on closeness to the outdoors, but also the timeliness and routine of ranch work that fell in step with the timeliness of days, weeks, months and seasons.

I was the lucky recipient of bed-sheets and towels scented from being laundered in Naptha bar soap in a wringer washer and hung in the sunshine to dry; also clothing impeccably starched, pressed and mended (if not also hand-sewn), and warm mittens and sweaters knitted by my mother's nimble fingers during quiet evenings while Daddy relaxed in a comfy chair after long hours of hard work. Meals were homecooked, largely from home-produced products: milk, cream and churned butter from the dairy cows, meat from the beef, and eggs and fried chicken on Sunday from Grandmother's chickens. Meals were consistently eaten accompanied by conversation three times a day, and all were hardy, to provide sustenance for hard-working men and growing children.

Though I didn't always participate in all the work involved here, I was aware of the processes and dedicated hours which went into our ranch/farm lifestyle. I saw the daily effort that over time produced irrigated fields, plentiful stacks of bailed hay and finally the end products of trucks loaded with piles of grain, well-fed beef cattle, or bags of wool sheared from sheep on the way to market. I sensed in the adults working together in families and community a strength of good character and pleasing smiles of self-fulfillment. It instilled in me a natural desire to want to do my best in whatever I pursued—homework, 4-H, piano practice, or contributing what I could to daily chores.

My children, who visited their grandparents on the ranch for a couple of weeks to a month during the summers of their youth, miss not having had the opportunity to create a ranch/farm lifestyle for their children—though some have creatively found ways to model the values they glimpsed during their Idaho visits. As I see more of the values instilled in the blessed farm/ranch lifestyle rapidly slipping away, my heart longs for days gone by.

*Lula and Bill Crane (front row) and their children:*
*Middle: Karen, Norene, Louise, Eve, Wilma, Ginger*
*Back: McKay, Melvin. Laurence, Tim*

*Eve, far left, with her precious "Gang-sisters"*
*Linda, Margaret, Polly June*
*Front: Vicki, Sharon, Marsha, ca 1970*
*Lana not pictured.*

## ACKNOWLEDGMENTS

*Some call it coming full circle; others serendipity. The Amish know it as an old-fashioned barn raising, where like minds and hearts, together, find joy in completing a most worthy project.*
*I call it the hand of the Lord, or Divine Determination.*

In the spring of 2021 Eve Dayton phoned our Arizona office to see if we might consider publishing the book you now have in your hand. At the time we were on such a treadmill I scarcely made note of her name while asking her to send a physical draft. As I congratulated her for getting her story on paper, our company was in the throes of a complicated yet exciting tome of an inspiring rags-to-riches gentleman we were researching in far away India. Our dance card was full for the better part of the year, but I promised we'd put her request in our consideration queue thereafter.

Eve promptly sent her manuscript; we perused it briefly and found it intriguing. A few months later we validated our interest to her by email but explained that we were unable to finalize acceptance.

We wished her good luck and bade her adieu.

What we had not digested fully was her last name: *Dayton*. Then we connected the dots. It was a name I had revered for forty-three years. When I was a single young woman and an aspiring actress in southern California, life had "happened" to me and I was seeking to change it. By Providence I met a man, his wife, children, and Christian congregation of friends that indeed exponentially transformed my soul from then until now. It so happened that Eve Dayton's brother-in-law,

*Richard and Linda Eyre with seven of their nine children, not long after the publisher met them.*

*Eve and Mark Dayton (in oval, back row right) with his siblings and their spouses including Elder L.Tom and Barbara Dayton Perry (front row, left) and Lyman and Elizabeth "Liz" Doty Dayton (second row, left).*

Lyman, and his wife Liz invited me into their home back then, where they taught and baptized me into the gospel of Jesus Christ and His path of peace.

Soon after, as the Lord would have it, I met another set of folks who would lift me to the next level. First was Ronald W. Reagan who asked me in 1979, along with many others, to help him become president of the United States. While answering his call, I met Harvard-educated Richard Eyre who also had been asked to assist with then-Governor Reagan's quest. Richard was an author of books I had grown to love during that first year in the Lord's Church. Two of my favorites were *What Manner of Man: A One-year Plan in Beginning to Know the Savior* and *Life Planning*, co-written with popular speaker and author Paul H. Dunn.

Once President Reagan was in office, Richard invited me to help him put together the White House Conference on Children, Youth, and Families. We aimed to promote the president's platform that the "traditional family is the basic unit of society." While working with Richard, his beautiful and brilliant wife Linda brought their little ones into the office on occasion to light up our day. Richard and Linda together would become prolific New York Times #1 bestselling authors and co-creators of the famous Joy Schools curriculum known the world over.

Not long after, I independently met, dated, and married a celebrated international journalist, Lee Roderick. Lee was also reared in Montpelier, Bear Lake Valley, Idaho, as was Richard's wife Linda. If that was not enough divine determination, on our wedding day Lee met Lyman Dayton, or rather, got reacquainted with him. Years earlier, when Lyman's father Reed led a large Montpelier/Cokeville, Wyoming-based Christian congregation, he called then-21-year-old Lee to serve a two-year mission in New Zealand. Connections with the Daytons and Eyres slowed for a time, until Eve's phone call on that spring day.

She was urged to reach out to me by her best friends, known affectionately as the "Gang-sisters," from their days together at Montpelier High School. They were Polly June Crane, Vicki Cochran, Lana Tippetts, Sharon Rowsell, Margaret Payne, Marsha Humphrey, and of course the wind beneath Eve's-to-be-published wings, Linda Jacobson. It was Linda who early on had given Eve my name as a possible publisher of interest and later provided the hurricane-strength energy and enthusiasm propelling this book into your hands.

When Linda connected with me last August she kindly asked if I might say "yes" and give a green light to this book. I gave the *only* right answer on the eve of Eve's going to heaven. Once our schedule opened up early in 2023, production of this book—as author Ross Peterson would say—became an absolute "labor of love." The devotion of Eve's friends and family made us fall in love with Eve without ever laying eyes on her.

Special thanks go to Polly, whose quickened fingers keyboarded a perfect electronic version of an early draft. Her wit guided this production journey with remarkable sensitivity. Vickie's Afterword is not only poignant but true. Heartfelt endorsements came from Lana, Sharon, and Margaret for which we are grateful. We are confident that another Gang-sister, the late Marsha Humphrey Brunett, encouraged Eve from upstairs, leading up to and during this pivotal year.

We also fell in love with the community-mindedness of Bear Lake/Montpelier/Bennington residents and families which still carry over from days gone by. We are deeply grateful to Ginger Crane Swensen, Eve's sister, and her massive collection of photo images, given to Schwabb-

Matthew's Chad Walker. True to the spirit of Bear Lake, and in a heartbeat, Chad filled our inbox with a plethora of high-resolution images pulled from the five-star video he created for Eve's memorial tribute; a few of which adorn these pages.

Folks from outside beautiful Bear Lake Valley have caught Eve's "fever" as well. At the top of the list is our designer-extraordinaire, Mickey Fryer, whose nimble hands and expert eye guided every single word, space, and image to this most attractive conclusion. The idea for and first set of branding irons which adorn most pages herein originated with Barbara "Bobbi" M. Snow, author of *Thousand Peaks Ranch: A Hundred Years of Stewardship*. Supremely talented and generous artist Robert Duncan gifted us another classic cover that makes *My Seventh Summer* a perfect companion piece to Ross Peterson's *Christmas in Montpelier*. In his set of memoirs, Ross reflected:

> *I love my hometown and its people. Some of the toughest, kindest, meanest, forgiving, and loving of God's human creations roamed [there]. Their children were my friends, and our fondness grows as time passes.*

As we revere this collective *barnraising*; the entire experience from my blessed early California days to Washington D.C. to the Intermountain West to the printing of Eve's masterpiece you hold in your hands, makes me "glad" that I married a "'Pelier boy." Lee's masterful editing ensured the author's original intent and panache were kept intact. And just for good measure, William Weaver—Lee's grand uncle—also had a sheep ranch in Bennington in the 1950s!

As publisher, I dedicate this book to all the Bear Lakers who have *shepherded* me to come full circle, shoulder to shoulder with the wonderful Dayton family, the amazing Eyre family, and now the remarkable Crane family that we learn so much about in Eve's pages. We are in awe of Father's Hand, His Divine Determination, which has guided the production of *My Seventh Summer: Tale of a Sheepman's Daughter* from the bery beginning: written by, crafted for, and honoring everything about Eve Idella Crane Dayton.

God bless you, the reader, for all the good you do and the stories within you. May you get them on paper and inspire us—as our friend and sister Eve has done so well.

*—Yvonne Maddox Roderick, publisher, Probitas Press*

www.ingramcontent.com/pod-product-compliance
Lightning Source LLC
LaVergne TN
LVHW090606110826
845146LV00001B/284

* 9 7 9 8 9 8 8 2 8 1 2 0 7 *